CAUGHT AT THE EDGE

The Birth of the New Frequencies

Caught At The Edge
The Birth of the New Frequencies

By Elizabeth Joyce

All rights reserved. This book, or parts thereof, may not be reproduced in any form without written permission from the publisher.

ISBN- 978-0-9972083-6-8

**Copyright
January 23, 2026**

Cover

Shutterstock from NASA

**All Bible quotes are from the
King James version (KJV)**

Publishing, Editing, and Page Layout by

Visions of Reality
21 Roslyn Ave.
Warner, NH. 03278

E-Mail: Elizabeth@new-visions.com

201-934-8986
answering service

Printed in the United States of America

ALSO BY ELIZABETH JOYCE

Books
Psychic Attack, Are You A Victim?

Ascension—Accessing The Fifth Dimension
Ascension—Accessing The Fifth Dimension Workbook

Opening To Your Intuition and Psychic Sensitivity
Developing Your Sixth Sense
BOOK ONE
BOOK TWO and
BOOK THREE

The New Spiritual Chakras
Unlimited Realities
Seeding and Nurturing the Garden of Your Soul
Backstage
Mysteries Revealed

CD Programs
Spiritual Healing and Meditation
Healing Depression the Natural Way
The Chakras and Your Body
Opening The Spiritual Chakras

All of the above items are available from Amazon.com,
Ingram, Book Stores, and
Visions of Reality

DEDICATION

To Caroline,
whose passing opened the first
great doorway of my life.
Your love, your courage, and your
quiet spiritual depth
set the foundation for everything
I would one day understand.

Even in your leaving,
you taught me how the soul continues—
how presence becomes Light,
and how love becomes a guide
that never fades.

You walk with me still, soft as breath,
strong as truth.

To Nilas,
my beloved foster son,
who followed his sister a year later,
carrying a soul far older than his years.
Your time here was gentle, bright, and sacred.

When you stepped beyond the veil,
the world did not grow darker—
it grew more transparent.
You remain with me in ways deeper

than memory, clearer than sight,
closer than heartbeat.

Your spirit stands beside mine
as I write every word of this book.

For both of you—Caroline and Nilas—
whose love lifted me,
whose departures transformed me,
and whose presence beyond the veil
continues to guide my path.

This book is yours.
Now and always.

Preface

There are periods in human history when change does not announce itself through sudden events, but through a quiet alteration of rhythm. Life begins to move differently. Time feels denser. Decisions seem to matter more quickly. The familiar pause between action and consequence narrows, and with it, our margin for unconsciousness. *Caught at the Edge* was written from within such a moment.

This book is not a forecast, nor an argument for belief. It is a record of awareness—an exploration of what it feels like to live at a threshold where established systems, inner and outer, are no longer sufficient on their own. The "edge" is not an external phenomenon waiting to arrive. It is the experiential boundary we cross when the pace of change outstrips our habitual ways of thinking, responding, and understanding.

Throughout history, symbolic systems have marked these periods of acceleration. Astrology, psychology, and spiritual traditions alike describe times when perception quickens, communication intensifies, and collective response becomes immediate. As air-dominant cycles come into prominence, movement shifts from matter to mind—from physical accumulation to mental, social, and informational velocity. Many have sensed this long before it became visible: that life would feel faster, more compressed, and less tolerant of delay. This book arises from that recognition.

At the turning of a year, I experienced a moment of awareness that did not arrive as explanation, but as understanding. It was not scientific information, nor knowledge intended to be proven. It was symbolic, precise, and instructional—offered in the way awareness often is, before language or mechanism can follow.

One image remains especially clear: the face of a clock. I did not understand this as a literal alteration of time, but as a revelation about compression. Less pause. Less buffer. Less distance between choice and outcome. What once unfolded gradually now responds more quickly. Time itself has not changed; our relationship to consequence has. This is not punishment. It is acceleration.

Acceleration, however, places new demands on consciousness. Without maturity, speed destabilizes. With discernment, it refines. The essential question of this era is not what is changing, but whether human awareness is prepared to meet change without reflexive fear, domination, or denial.

The chapters that follow explore this question through lived experience, psychological insight, and spiritual reflection. They do not ask the reader to accept extraordinary claims, but to recognize familiar patterns: the impulse to control what is not understood, the discomfort that arises when certainty dissolves, and the challenge of responding wisely when events move faster than interpretation.

If there is a warning contained here, it is a quiet one: the luxury of unconscious delay is ending. Wisdom must now keep pace with knowledge. Awareness must precede reaction.
This book is offered in that spirit.
Not to alarm, but to steady.
Not to predict, but to orient.
Not to persuade, but to invite clarity.
We are not approaching the edge.
We are learning how to stand upon it.

TABLE OF CONTENTS

DEDICATION   iv

Preface   vi

Prelude *At the Threshold*   xvii
A quiet, unseen shift passes through the field of Earth, unnoticed by most, felt deeply by a few, marking the threshold of a turning that has already begun.

Chapter 1 *The First Sign*   Pg. 1
A faint, impossible object appears. Three strangers, across continents, recognize the same truth: something has entered human reality with intention.

Chapter 2 *The First Shadows Of Truth*   Pg. 11
At Mauna Kea Observatory, data deepens into disturbance. Observation gives way to recognition as the object reveals coherence.

Chapter 3 *Monika's Remote Vision.*   Pg. 21
Monika follows the resonance beyond instrumentation and encounters the object directly. What she receives is not data, but remembrance.

Chapter 4 *Harmonies In The Dark.*   Pg. 29
The object begins to communicate through structure and sound. As geometric harmonics form with deliberate precision, it becomes clear the signals are not meant for machines alone. A deeper alignment is underway.

**Chapter 5 *The Night of The First Window*
                                                        Pg. 37**
Nilas becomes consciously aware of the object's presence. Journalism gives way to destiny as observation becomes participation.

Chapter 6 *The Alignment Begins.*   Pg. 45
Planetary, human, and cosmic fields begin to align. Subtle changes ripple through perception and biology.

Chapter 7 *The First Witnesses*   Pg, 53
Nilas becomes consciously aware of the object's presence. Journalism gives way to destiny as observation becomes participation.

Chapter 8 *The Second Golden Window* Pg. 59
A stronger energetic threshold opens, marked by precise timing and increased coherence. Resonance intensifies. The object shifts from signaling to preparation, revealing deliberate timing.

Chapter 9 *The Awakening Of Nilas*   **Pg. 67**
Nilas crosses from observer to participant as his consciousness opens to the field he has been tracking.

Chapter 10 *The World Pauses*   **Pg. 77**
A collective stillness settles across the planet. Humanity senses a threshold without yet understanding it.

Chapter 11 *The First Departures.*   **Pg. 85**
A quiet global wave of crossings begins. Souls who have completed their cycles leave gently and without fear.

Chapter 12 *The Prophecy Line.*   **Pg. 93**
A luminous energetic pathway forms between Earth and the object. Monika translates its message: prepare, remember, awaken.

Chapter 13 *When The Soul Begins To Leave.*
                              Pg. 101
The departures continue. Grief and grace coexist as humanity realizes this is not loss, but transition.

Chapter 14 — *The Third Golden Window*
                              Pg.109
The object turns fully toward Earth. The final energetic window opens. The object prepares for descent as Earth's field stabilizes.

Chapter 15 — *The Night of The Turning*.
                                                              Pg, 117
A global stillness descends. Earth's old timeline collapses. The planetary field rotates into coherence.

Chapter 16 — The Descent Begins   Pg. 129
The object slows and synchronizes with Earth's magnetics and consciousness, initiating controlled entry.

Chapter 17 — *The Impact Over the Barents Sea*
                                                              Pg. 145
The object activates over the Barents Sea in a non-destructive, luminous event. The object enters Earth's field without destruction, activating a planetary shift in awareness.

Chapter 18 — *The Day After*   Pg. 155
Humanity begins to experience the immediate consequences of the shift. Fear diminishes. Awareness sharpens. The world feels unfamiliar and lighter.

Chapter 19 — *Communities of Light*   Pg. 163
New societies form organically through resonance rather than authority. Humanity begins to reorganize itself.

Chapter 20 — *The Still Point*   **Pg. 171**
Time, explanation, and movement pause.
Humanity reaches the zero point — the pause
where all timelines converge and conscious choice
becomes possible.

Chapter 21 — *The First Council of Unity*
                                                Pg. 175
Life resumes through embodiment. Michael is
born calmly and consciously into the new field,
carrying continuity rather than exception.
Ancestral presence affirms lineage and completion.

Chapter 22 — *Love Incarnates and*
                 Life Continues   **Pg. 181**
Marriage without spectacle.
Michael's birth anchors the future.

Chapter 23 — *The Council of Nine*   **Pg. 187**
Human society reorganizes without authority or
ideology. A council forms without hierarchy or
force, guided by resonance and shared
responsibility.

Chapter 23 — *The Way Forward*   **Pg. 193**
The future opens. Humanity steps into a new era
not defined by fear, but by remembrance and
choice. The world moves on—awake

About The Author   **Pg. 199**

ACKNOWLEDGEMENTS

To the Universe,
for its endless orchestration of Light
and shadow,
for the unseen geometry
that guides our journeys,
and for the cosmic intelligence that holds
every soul in its vast, loving embrace.

To the Galaxy,
our spiraling mother,
whose arms cradle billions of worlds—
some awakening, some resting,
some remembering what humanity
is just beginning to recall.
Your ancient wisdom ripples through
the stars and sings through every particle
of our being.

To our Solar System,
the radiant family in which we were born.

To the Sun,
whose light carries codes of memory
and evolution.

To the Planets,
each holding a fragment of the greater
octave of consciousness.
To the moons and magnetic fields

that steady us when we lose our center.
You are the silent guardians
of our unfolding.

To this struggling planet Earth,
our beloved, wounded, magnificent home.
You who have endured the weight
of human forgetfulness,
the scars of our mistakes,
and the pain of our separation from you,
yet still offer us air to breathe,
water to drink,
and beauty to nourish the soul.

Your oceans hold our history.
Your mountains hold our ancestors.
Your forests hold our healing.
Your patience has been immeasurable,
your forgiveness is without limit.

Thank you for allowing us another chance
to remember who we are,
why we came,
and how to live in harmony with all life.

To the unseen helpers,
the ancestors, guides, and interstellar kin
who gather at the edges of perception
and whisper just enough truth
to lead us toward our next step.
Your presence is subtle but unmistakable.

To the great Arc of Creation,
the living pulse that moves through
all worlds,
all hearts,
all time—
thank you for the privilege of listening
to even one small stanza
of your eternal music.

PRELUDE

At the Threshold

There are periods in human history when change does not announce itself through sudden catastrophe, but through a quiet alteration of rhythm. Life begins to move differently. Time feels denser. Decisions seem to carry weight more quickly. The familiar pause between action and consequence narrows, and with it, humanity's margin for unconsciousness. This was such a time.

The world did not feel as though it were ending. It felt as though it were approaching something—an invisible boundary where the old methods of understanding no longer held. People sensed it in subtle ways: a restlessness beneath daily routines, an intensification of dreams, a growing awareness that events no longer unfolded gradually but arrived all at once, demanding response.

Caught at the Edge is written from within that threshold. It is not a forecast, nor an argument for belief. It is a record of awareness—an exploration of what it feels like to live at a moment when systems, inner and outer, begin to outpace the structures that once contained them. The "edge" is not an external phenomenon waiting to arrive. It is the experiential boundary crossed when perception accelerates faster than habit, and consciousness is asked to mature in real time.

Throughout history, symbolic systems have marked such periods of acceleration. Astrology, psychology, and spiritual traditions alike describe moments when the collective field shifts toward speed— movement from matter to mind, from accumulation to immediacy. Air-dominant eras have always carried this signature. Thought quickens. Communication intensifies. Consequence shortens its distance from choice.

Many sensed this long before it became visible.

At the turning of a year, an awareness arrived—not as explanation, but as recognition. It did not present itself as scientific data, nor as information meant to be proven. It arrived symbolically, precisely, and instructionally, as awareness often does before language can follow.

One image remained especially clear: the face of a clock.

It was not understood as a literal alteration of time, but as compression. Less pause. Less buffer. Less distance between intention and outcome. Time itself had not changed; humanity's relationship to consequence had.

This was not punishment. It was acceleration.

Acceleration, however, places new demands on consciousness. Without discernment, speed destabilizes. With maturity, it refines. The essential question of this era was not what was changing, but whether human awareness was prepared to meet change without fear, domination, or denial.

The pages that follow explore this moment through lived experience—psychological, observational, and reflective. They do not ask the reader to accept extraordinary claims, but to recognize familiar patterns: the impulse to control what is not yet understood, the discomfort that arises when certainty dissolves, and the challenge of responding wisely when events move faster than interpretation.

If there is a warning contained here, it is a quiet one: the luxury of unconscious delay is ending. Awareness must now precede reaction. Wisdom must keep pace with knowledge.

This book is offered in that spirit.

Not to alarm, but to steady.
Not to predict, but to orient.
Not to persuade, but to invite clarity.

We are not approaching the *edge*.

We are learning how to stand upon it.

CHAPTER ONE
The First Sign

The first sign did not arrive with sirens. It arrived with a shift in rhythm so slight most people moved through it without noticing, the way the body forgets a pressure change until a headache blooms hours later. The world continued to rotate. Screens continued to glow. Planes crossed the sky. Children slept.

And yet, something in the field of Earth—beneath weather and politics and noise—tilted. Those who were attuned felt it first. Not as fear. As recognition.

It is difficult to describe the beginning of a turning, because it does not announce itself as an event. It announces itself as a pattern. A coherence. A quiet alignment that enters reality the way a thought enters the mind before words can form.

There had been a moment like that before.

March 23, 2025.

Most people never heard of it. No headlines. No alerts. No public record that mattered to daily life. But in certain observatories, archived measurements later showed a brief and statistically improbable curvature—an alignment that was not a line but a bow, as though the solar system itself had turned its face toward something not yet visible.

Monika Adler stood at her kitchen window in Munich that night, holding a cup of tea she forgot to drink.

She was not watching the sky in the ordinary sense. She was listening. She had spent a lifetime learning the difference between imagination and perception, between anxiety and a true signal. She knew what it felt like when the mind created, and she knew what it felt like when something else moved through her.

That night the air in the room became precise. It was not quiet. It was precise.

Her short blond hair, neatly styled to frame her striking features, lifted faintly as if the atmosphere had changed pressure. The sensation tightened beneath her sternum, not painful, simply insistent, as though an invisible hand had pressed a fingertip against the center of her chest and said: *remember this*.

She did not see planets "move." She felt a curvature in the field. gesture. A response. No one had language for it. Not yet. Monika whispered a single sentence into the glass. "It has begun." She did not know what "it" was. Only that the world had crossed a threshold.

Months passed. Life resumed its ordinary insistence. But the field did not forget. Then, in July 2025, the first sign arrived. It came first as a faint point of light—so dim and erratic it might have been dismissed as noise if the instruments had not been as patient as the people operating them. It appeared briefly on deep-space arrays. Disappeared. Returned. Adjusted its track in a way that felt too clean to be accidental.

At Mauna Kea Station on Hawaii Island, Dr. Reza Karimi leaned toward a monitor and narrowed his eyes. The control room hummed softly; the slow fan of cooling systems, the steady vibration of tracking gears, and the quiet breath of electronics that never slept. The smell of coffee lingered in the recycled air.

Reza's dark hair was slightly disheveled from another long shift. His glasses reflected pale green telemetry as his fingers moved across the console with practiced precision.

He magnified the capture. The object sat near the bottom of the screen like a stubborn thought. "That's not ours," he murmured.

His assistant glanced up from the secondary console, a cup of instant ramen steaming beside her elbow. "A reflection? Sensor echo?"

Reza shook his head slowly. "No meteor curve. No expected entry vector." He rotated the spectral overlay again, fingers tightening slightly on the controls. "And it's coming from north of the ecliptic." The words settled into the room. That was wrong. Everything in their training said that was wrong.

His assistant swallowed. "Could it be an unlogged satellite?"

Reza didn't answer immediately. He pulled up the back-projection model and ran the vector outward, not forward in time, but backward through space. The line extended past the planetary plane, past the familiar clutter of near-Earth objects, past the outer limits of the solar neighborhood entirely. It did not terminate.

His jaw tightened. "That trajectory doesn't stay local," he said quietly. "It's inbound from above the galactic plane."

He adjusted the scale again. The projection narrowed, converging toward the inner regions of the Milky Way, a dense, star-rich direction instruments rarely traced cleanly.

The assistant stared at the screen. "You mean… interstellar?"

Reza felt a pressure in his chest he couldn't explain; not fear, not excitement, but the unmistakable sensation of contact.

"Yes," he said, "and deliberate." He watched the data refresh. Watched the object correct its course by a fraction of a degree. It was not drifting, not tumbling, but adjusting.

"Nothing else drifts in that manner," he observed quietly, directing the remark more to himself than to her. He did not know why the next word came out of his mouth, but once it did, he could not pull it back. "This is… deliberate."

Across the ocean, Monika woke as if someone had called her name. Her apartment was dim.

Moonlight cut a pale bar across the quilt at her feet. The room smelled faintly of lavender and old books, but tonight the air carried an edge with it; charged, as if the atmosphere had inhaled and was holding its breath.

She sat up and pressed a hand to her sternum. The same place. The same pressure. A frequency moved inside her body. It was not sound, not emotion, but something subtler; a sub-threshold vibration that traveled through bone and blood like a message delivered through structure rather than language.

She closed her eyes and visualized the scene. A faint spark was moving through the dark of interstellar space, curving toward the solar system with unmistakable intention.

Monika was not an astronomer. She was an intuitive, a remote viewer, a quiet empath who had spent her life learning to trust what arrived within her inner sight, without explanation. She had never wished for drama. She had never chased mystery.

However, the image was too clear to dismiss. "It's coming," she whispered. Her voice did not tremble. Her hands did. But from where, she thought. The answer did not arrive. Only the knowing that something had entered the field.

Something ancient, coherent, and impossibly important.

In Reykjavik, Iceland, Nilas Von Eckenberg sat alone in a rooftop greenhouse while the city slept beneath a cover of winter sky. The glass structure was warm despite the northern cold. The room was humid with basil and mint, the faint sweetness of tomato vines, and the steady drip of irrigation that sounded like patient time. Snow piled in soft drifts against the outside walls, muting the night into an almost sacred stillness.

Nilas was a journalist by trade and a seeker by nature. He was tall, steady, with the quiet strength of a man who listened for patterns others ignored. His laptop glowed on the wooden table in front of him. With his soft blue eyes, he had been staring at a blank document for nearly an hour, unsettled by a feeling he could not name.

An email pinged. Subject line: Unclassified object. Off-path. Need eyes.

Nilas opened the attachment. A blurred, low-resolution capture appeared; nothing more than a faint spark suspended in black. It should have meant nothing. It should have been another piece of internet speculation or a half-baked lead.

But the moment he saw it, his stomach tightened. Not fear. Recognition. As if he were seeing a photograph of someone he once knew in another life. He whispered, "Where did you come from?" He printed the image, pinned it to the corkboard above his desk, and circled it once with a pen that shook slightly in his hand.

Then he circled it again. Something in him wanted to make the object real by marking it. Wanted to claim it as a story. Wanted, more frighteningly, to find it.

Back at Mauna Kea, Reza reran the telemetry. Hours had passed. Morning was approaching. The control room was colder now, fluorescent lights flickering faintly overhead. Only three staff remained, all hunched over monitors in exhausted silence.

Reza checked the object's path against archived data and stopped abruptly. A faint curvature appeared behind the object. A subtle geometric line unlike any tail or debris trail he had seen in twenty years. He enlarged it. Adjusted contrast. Overlaid it against old measurements.

His throat went dry. "It's an arc," he whispered.

His assistant frowned. "A trail?"

"No." Reza's voice became small, as if the room had grown too large. "Not a trail." He pulled up the archived file.

March 23, 2024. There it was, quietly recorded, never publicized, dismissed at the time as statistical oddity. The brief curvature of planetary geometry. The shape behind the object mirrored it.

Reza felt a shiver crawl up his spine. "It's following the arc curvature," he breathed. "Like it was summoned." The word summoned should have embarrassed him. It belonged to myth, not instrumentation. But he could not unsee what the data showed.

Across the world, Monika sat at her kitchen table, a cup of tea cooling between her trembling fingers. Her apartment was silent, yet the frequency inside her body pulsed stronger, clearer. Her remote-viewer's mind kept locking onto the same image: a luminous seed; hollow, not empty but full of potential, wrapped in volatile crystalline gases that shimmered like liquid starlight.

Nilas stared at the printed image until his eyes watered. He began to write in his notebook, not an article, not a report, but a question he could not stop asking. Why do I feel like I'm supposed to find you?

None of them knew what the faint spark truly was. None understood its purpose, or why it had entered the solar system along the same curvature the sky itself had traced months before. But all of them felt the same underlying truth, scientist, intuitive, journalist. This was not random. This was not a mistake. This was not merely a visitor in space. Something had entered human reality, not benign or malevolent, but catalytic.

And the first sign had appeared.

CHAPTER TWO
The First Shadows of Truth

By morning, the Hale Pōhaku facility on Mauna Kea was buzzing, not loudly, but with a quiet intensity. No one shouted, no one ran, but the air carried a feeling of a collective inhale waiting for permission to exhale. The building itself seemed to hum; the soft click of cooling metal, the faint whir of processors under strain, the drifting scent of old coffee and cold mountain air that seeped in through the sliding doors.

Monika had not planned to be there. She had arrived on a late flight from Munich less than twelve hours earlier, summoned not by certainty but by the quiet insistence that had followed her since March. Reza Karimi's message had been brief—unusual data, unfamiliar harmonics, a request framed carefully as consultation rather than belief. She had not asked who else would be present. Some questions answered themselves when the moment arrived. She could feel the tension in the way people moved; precise, uneasy, purposeful. Everyone sensed it, even if they couldn't name it.

Nilas stood near the central console, scribbling notes in his dark leather journal, credentials clipped to his jacket, access granted through channels he rarely named out loud. The warm greenhouse scent of his clothes, earth, pine, basil, still clung to him from his life in Iceland. He wrote quickly, not as a reporter filing facts, but as someone desperate to capture the *feeling* of the moment before it slipped through his fingers like mist.

Kai watched him with a softened smile. He had been present since before the shift, before the data drew names and credentials into the room. Standing near the wide glass window, his silhouette framed by the pale morning light, Kai appeared calm. Too calm for the atmosphere around him. *Nilas sees with two eyes,* Kai thought. *The physical and the inward.*

Monika returned to her station, her short blond hair pinned back beneath a lightweight headset, thin-framed glasses perched on her nose. Her fingers hovered above the keyboard, though she already knew the numbers by heart. They had burned into her mind the moment they appeared.

Trajectory direct. Rotation deliberate. Harmonics structured. Origin unknown. She ran the deep-scan again. Same result. No drift. No chaos. No orbital decay. Her pulse quickened. Her chest tightened.

A secure notification followed minutes later—verification from Chile, accompanied by coordinates and motion vectors, directing Mauna Kea's arrays toward the Sagittarius sector above the ecliptic

Nilas tilted his head, studying her expression with those clear, sensitive hazel eyes. "You're troubled," he said quietly.

"I'm focused."

"That isn't what I asked."

She paused her typing, surprised and unsettled by his clarity. "What do you think I'm troubled about?"

He closed the journal, leaning against the console with that steady, grounded presence that made him seem carved from the Earth itself. "That it's not behaving like anything we understand." A beat. "And that part of you recognizes it."

Her breath stilled.

Kai stepped forward, his voice gentle.

"He's right, Monika."

She ignored the heat rising in her chest. "Recognizing isn't the word."

Nilas's voice softened. "Then what is?"

Monika looked back at the screen as the object drifted across the display, a faint pulse of light riding the darkness like a coded whisper. "It feels," she said, her voice growing faint, "familiar."

Kai nodded. "Because you are sensing its field."

Nilas stepped closer. "Field?"

Kai did not look away from the screen.

"Everything conscious has a field. Humans. Animals. Planets. Even certain objects. When you align with another field, something moves between you."

Nilas whispered, "Information?"

"Recognition," Kai corrected.

Monika tightened her grip on the edge of the console. "It's just data. We're reading too much into it."

But Nilas heard the tension in her voice—the quiver behind her certainty.

He could read her more easily than she liked.

Across the room, another analyst called out, "Monika! You need to see this."

She hurried over, her shoes clicking sharply against the cold tile floor.

A new harmonic signature had appeared overnight. It was faint—a soft rise and fall in perfect intervals—too clean to be natural.

Nilas stood behind her, close enough that she felt his presence at her back. "Is that... a pattern?"

"It's repeating," she said, her voice tightening. "Every seven minutes."

"Why seven?" Nilas asked.

Kai answered without looking up. "Because seven signals consciousness awakening."

The words made no logical sense, yet Monika felt the hum beneath her sternum again, the same soft pull she'd felt the moment she first sensed the object.

She whispered, "It's increasing its resonance."

Nilas swallowed. "To what end?"

Kai answered calmly, as if the truth had been sitting beside him all along. "To prepare humanity."

A chill rippled down Nilas's spine. "Prepare for… what?"

Kai turned to them both, expression gentle, yet firm, as though bracing them for the truth. "For what is coming."

Monika inhaled slowly, trying to steady the rising electricity inside her.

Across the room, the harmonic line suddenly spiked. A sharp pulse of light flickered across the monitors like a heartbeat from across the void.

Nilas leaned closer. "What was that?"

Monika typed rapidly, her fingers trembling as she recalibrated the spectrometer. "It's communicating," she murmured.

Nilas froze. "Communicating with what?"

She hesitated.

Kai answered for her. "With the Sun."

Nilas stared. "The Sun?"

"Yes." Kai stepped to the window, gazing at the dim horizon as the early light stretched across the mountain. "It's speaking to our star, and the Sun is responding."

Monika turned sharply. "Kai, how can you possibly know that?"

Kai's voice was calm, ancient, steady. "Because the universe speaks through energy. Through resonance. Through vibration and rhythm. Your instruments translate those rhythms into numbers. But numbers are only symbols. The truth is older."

Nilas watched Monika's reaction. She wasn't dismissing Kai. She wasn't resisting. She was listening to every word.

He realized then that Monika wasn't afraid of the object. She was afraid of what she already knew.

She exhaled slowly. "If it's communicating," she said, "then it's not just passing through."

"No," Kai replied softly. "It isn't passing through."

Nilas opened his journal and wrote one quiet sentence: *It's coming to us.*

Monika brushed a loose strand of hair from her face and straightened her posture. "We need more data. More scans. More—"

Kai interrupted gently.

"Monika… sometimes the truth is not in the data."

Nilas added in a low voice, "Sometimes the truth is in the feeling."

The harmonic pulse flashed again—brighter this time. The object had heard them.

Monika closed her eyes for a moment, feeling the resonance rise inside her—not a warning, not fear, but a deep, ancient knowing settling in her chest like a memory.

Nilas saw her expression shift. Softly, he whispered, "What is it?"

She opened her eyes, steady now. "It's accelerating."

Kai stepped beside them, his presence a calm pillar amidst the tension. "And this," he said quietly, "is only the beginning."

Monika stared at the screen as the light pulsed once more; steady, deliberate, alive. Somewhere beyond the edge of human sight, across the dark canvas of space, the object continued its impossible approach.

Nilas whispered the words none of them wanted to speak aloud: "It's coming straight for us."

Caught At The Edge

CHAPTER THREE
Monika's Remote Vision

Monika hadn't planned to stay late. The others had drifted out of the observatory one by one, silhouettes disappearing into the soft violet dusk that clung to the mountaintop. The air was thin and cool at this altitude, scented faintly with stone dust and the metallic tang of the telescope arrays cooling for the night. Silence wrapped the building like a second atmosphere.

Only Nilas lingered. He sat in a corner near a wall of observation screens, his long frame folded easily into the chair, journal balanced against his knee. The warm glow of a small desk lamp softened the angles of his face and reflected off the slight sheen of moisture on the greenhouse soil still trapped beneath his boots.

He wrote continuously, not even glancing down, as though the words were selecting him rather than the other way around. He looked up when she stood. "You're not done," he said gently, his voice calm, aware.

"No," she admitted. "I'm not."

Before she could take another step, Kai appeared, emerging from the dim hallway with the serenity of someone who never truly arrived or left a room. His presence always felt predestined, as though he existed in the space between moments. "You're feeling the pull," he said.

Monika tensed, shoulders rising slightly. "I'm feeling the responsibility."

Kai's mouth curved in a soft, knowing smile. "Responsibility is the mind's word. The soul feels recognition."

Nilas closed his journal slowly. He studied Monika with quiet intensity, not intrusively, but with the sensitivity of someone who had spent his life listening for what most people never said aloud. He had felt it earlier, in that exact moment when the harmonic signature changed, Monika's breathing had shifted, her energy subtly opening as though answering a familiar voice. She turned away before either man could see the flicker of truth in her eyes.

Monika returned to her console, her hands trembling slightly as she reactivated the interface. Blue light spilled across her face, illuminating her delicate features: The high cheekbones, the focused hazel eyes, the tension she tried so hard to hide.

She zoomed in on the object's present location, still faint, still small, pulsing with that rhythmic, deliberate glow that felt like a whisper lodged beneath her heart.

Nilas rose and stepped closer, his presence warm and steady beside her. "What are you sensing?" he asked softly.

She didn't look at him. "I'm not sensing anything. I'm analyzing."

He hesitated, reading the micro-shift in her posture. "Monika... sometimes your analysis looks a lot like intuition."

Her breath caught with a small, involuntary intake. The truth pressed too close.

Kai stepped nearer, folding his hands behind his back in a posture that radiated patience. "Monika," he said gently, "you were born remembering things this world forgets."

She froze. The words struck a deep, dormant chord in her. A memory without an image, an understanding without a source.

Nilas saw it in her eyes, saw the burn of recognition widening behind her calm surface. "What does that mean?" he asked, voice low.

Kai did not answer him. He kept his gaze on Monika alone.

"You've done remote viewing since childhood," he said. "You see structures, patterns, intentions that instruments cannot detect. You've always known your sight was not just mental."

Monika's throat tightened. "That was imagination," she murmured.

"No." Kai's voice softened into something almost musical. "It was memory."

Her knees softened. She gripped the console to ground herself.

Nilas touched her elbow, not restraining, not overtaking, but anchoring her.

Monika closed her eyes, letting her breath settle. She wasn't afraid. She wasn't overwhelmed. She was remembering

Kai stepped back slightly, giving her space without distance.

"Sit," he said softly.

She sat.

"Now breathe."

She obeyed.

The hum beneath her sternum, the resonance she had tried to ignore grew warmer, steadier, more insistent.

Nilas watched every movement, his pulse quickening unexpectedly. It felt as though he had been waiting for this moment his entire life, without knowing what "this moment" would be.

Kai's voice lowered into a tone that felt older than language. "Follow the pull."

Monika inhaled.

"Follow it past the numbers," Kai whispered. "Past the instruments. Past the mind."

Her heartbeat slowed.

The room dissolved into a soft blur. Nilas's presence hovered to her left; a warm, protective field. Kai's presence stood behind her right shoulder ancient, steady, anchoring. And the resonance—the resonance became a doorway.

A gentle pressure opened behind her eyes, as though an inner lens had begun to rotate toward the cosmos. Not outward, but inward—into memory. Into recognition. A flash.

Monika gasped quietly. She wasn't in the room. She was out there. Floating near the dark object, watching as its fissures glowed with an inner golden light. The vapor streams curled around it like living geometry, humming with a rhythm that felt like a heartbeat in slow motion.

She drifted closer. Closer. The object turned. *Toward her.* A pulse of energy rippled outward. It was not a warning. It felt like a greeting. A remembrance. Her hand reached into the vision — though her physical body remained still in the chair.

Nilas whispered urgently, "She's seeing something."

Kai nodded. "It's okay. Let her."

Another pulse surged outward, soft and luminous, like starlight bending into intention.

A whisper: *You know us.*

Monika's breath shuddered.

Another whisper: *We remember you.*

Her eyes flew open. She inhaled sharply, gripping the armrest as though anchoring herself in her body again.

Nilas leaned closer, alarmed. "Monika—?"

She raised a trembling hand.

"I saw it," she whispered. "I saw the fissure. The geometry. The… the energy."

Nilas swallowed, his voice barely audible. "What did it say?"

Monika met his gaze, her voice trembling. "It said it remembers me."

Nilas stared, the truth sinking deep into his bones like cold water.

Kai stepped forward, his expression gentler than ever before. "It's because you were meant to understand it."

Monika pressed a hand to her chest, still shaking as the resonance slowly softened within her.

Nilas's voice was steady, almost reverent. "What does it want?"

She shook her head slowly. "I don't know." But she did. She felt it.

Kai finished the thought for her: "It wants to awaken humanity."

Silence filled the observatory. A silence of gravity. A silence of truth.

Outside, the night sky stretched endlessly across the mountaintop like a dark canvas waiting for its next brushstroke. Somewhere across that vastness, the object pulsed softly, as though answering Monika's breath.

This was no longer observation. This was a beginning.

CHAPTER FOUR
Harmonies in the Dark

The observatory always felt different at night. During the day it carried the familiar energy of human minds—busy, analytical, determined to pin the universe into columns of numbers. But after midnight, when the valley sank into silence and the world below the mountain fell asleep, the building no longer belonged to the scientists who worked inside it. It belonged to the sky.

Tonight, the sky was restless. A cold breeze drifted through the seam of the loading bay door, bringing with it the scent of pine and volcanic stone. The domed ceiling above them creaked faintly as the temperature dropped. Somewhere outside, a hawk gave a distant cry, its wings carving through a field of stars.

Monika returned to the central console as the interior lights dimmed into the soft indigo glow of night mode. The screens lit her face with gentle pulses of shifting blue light, highlighting the concentration etched across her brow.

A soft flicker caught her attention. A pulse. Blue-white. Rhythmic. Deliberate. Her heartbeat quickened.

Nilas entered quietly behind her, the faint scent of snow and wind clinging to his jacket. His hair was still slightly damp from the fog outside, and the glow of the monitors caught in his ice-blue eyes. He didn't speak—he rarely did when she was in this state of deep focus. Something in him recognized the fragile tension she carried, and he instinctively matched it, his breath soft, his presence gentle.

Kai stood at the far end of the room, hands folded behind his back, eyes half-closed. He resembled someone listening for a sound older than memory, as if the harmonics themselves were whispering directly into his bones.

The console chimed softly. Monika frowned. "It's happening again."

Nilas moved closer, his boots silent on the cold tile. "Another pulse?"

"Worse," she said. "Something new." The harmonic line across the spectrum display had begun to bend—not in the chaotic swing of ~~noise, but~~ noise but curling into a shape that made no physical sense. A spiral. A perfect, mathematical spiral.

Light swirling inside data. Nilas whispered, "Is that natural?"

"No," she replied instantly. "Nothing about this is natural."

Kai's eyes opened. "Geometry is always the first language," he said quietly.

Monika glanced at him. "First language of what?"

"Of consciousness."

Before she could respond, the spectroscope chimed three tones, soft and even, like a distant bell tolling in the dark. The screen brightened. The spiral expanded outward, layering itself into a double arc. Monika adjusted the filters, fingers flying across the keys. Her breath hitched when the new geometry came into focus. "What… is it doing?"

Nilas leaned closer, the tension in his voice unmistakable. "It looks like it's forming a pattern."

Kai approached them with slow, measured steps, his presence calming the air around them. "It is forming a message."

Monika froze. "Messages require intent."

Kai nodded. "Yes."

Nilas's breath caught. "Then, you're saying it's trying to communicate?"

"Not trying," Kai said softly. "Communicating."

Monika swallowed, her pulse thudding beneath her ribs. "It shouldn't be able to do this at such a distance…"

A second chime—five tones joined the first. A new line appeared beneath the spiral. Thin, elegant, utterly precise.

Nilas murmured, "What is that?"

Monika zoomed in, her hands trembling slightly. "It's… harmonic layering. But it shouldn't be possible at this distance."

"Distance," Kai said softly, "is irrelevant."

A sharp frustration flashed behind Monika's eyes. "No, distance defines resonance response. For it to generate this level of harmonic complexity, it would need—" She stopped.

Nilas stepped forward. "What?"

Her voice fell to a whisper. "It would need to know we're listening."

Silence fell over the observatory, heavy and charged.

Kai stepped closer to the console. He lifted his hand a few inches above the display, as if sensing the energy radiating from the spiral itself. "The object is aligning," he said. "Slowly. Deliberately."

Nilas's voice deepened with awe. "Aligning with what?"

Kai looked directly at Monika. "With her."

Nilas turned sharply.

Monika stepped back, her pulse spiking. "No. No. You can't know that."

"I can," Kai said. "You felt the resonance. The vision. The recognition."

Monika's throat tightened. "But that doesn't mean—"

Another pulse burst across the screen—bright, clean, rhythmic. Seven tones. Seven perfectly spaced harmonic peaks rising like a ladder into the dark. Nilas grabbed the back of a chair to steady himself. "It's the number seven again."

Kai nodded. "Awakening." She forced herself to breathe evenly. "If it keeps rising like this, the next harmonic could overwhelm our sensors."

Nilas asked, "What happens then?"

"We lose the feed." Kai added, "Temporarily."

Monika stiffened. "Why temporarily?"

Kai's voice lowered, ancient and steady. "Because the next harmonic will not be for the machines."

Nilas's voice shook. "Who will it be for?"

Kai turned toward Monika. "For her."

Her breath hitched, sharp and immediate. The screens flared—a wash of soft gold light spreading across every monitor. The harmonic spiral widened, turning from shape into motion; alive, breathing, pulsing in a rhythm that matched the thrum beneath Monika's sternum.

Nilas whispered, "Monika...?"

The pull returned, stronger than before,
as if something inside her had finally awakened
and recognized a frequency that belonged to her.

She whispered, barely audible: "It's calling." The entire room hummed.

Kai closed his eyes.

Nilas took her hand without thinking—instinctively protective, grounding her as though drawn by something deeper than choice.

She didn't pull away.

The harmonics rose again, forming a third spiral, a perfect geometry. So ancient it hummed in the bones.

Kai's voice trembled—not with fear, but reverence. "This is the Sign of Approach."

Nilas turned to him. "Approach of what?"

Kai answered without looking away from the spirals. "The moment when the object begins to reveal its purpose."

Monika stared at the golden threads weaving themselves into a living shape, a shape that felt more like *memory* than mathematics. She exhaled slowly. "This is only the beginning." The harmonic pattern pulsed hard—one final echo—before fading into silence. For a moment, the room became utterly still.

Nilas tightened his grip on her hand. Kai breathed deeply, as though absorbing a sacred truth.

Monika whispered into the quiet: "It knows we're here." And somewhere in the star-black dark, the object hummed back.

CHAPTER FIVE
Night of the First Window

The night of the first golden window arrived quietly, no storms, no seismic shifts, no cosmic roar. Just a stillness so profound it felt like the universe was inhaling. The world had no idea what was coming.

But Monika felt it the instant the Sun sank beneath the horizon. A subtle pressure gathered behind her breastbone, not fear, not warning, but anticipation. Something was aligning in the heavens, in the energetic field, and inside her.

The observatory lights dimmed automatically as the mountain surrendered to darkness. Outside the glass-encased walls, the sky unfolded into a dome of sharpened starlight, silver pinpoints trembling in the thin, cold air. The wind brushed softly over the metal framework, bringing with it the scent of volcanic stone and frost.

Nilas stood near the panoramic glass wall, his tall, slight figure silhouetted against the velvet sky. His posture was still, rooted, contemplative, like a quiet scribe watching the beginning of a prophecy he did not yet understand, but instinctively recognized. He spoke without turning. "It begins tonight."

Monika joined him, their reflections barely visible in the darkened glass. "What makes you say that?"

Nilas exhaled, fogging the window. "Because the sky feels awake."

Before she could respond, Kai entered from the far corridor with fluid, silent steps. He seemed to glide rather than walk, his presence shifting the air itself. Soft light seemed to halo around him, as though the darkness bent gently out of his way. "The first window will open in seven minutes," he said.

Monika's breath caught. "Seven minutes? Our next scan isn't until…"

"Schedules," Kai said gently, "are for moments born of logic. This moment is born of alignment."

Nilas nodded with quiet certainty. "The number seven again."

Monika moved to her console, her fingers already dancing over the controls. The telescope shifted on its great mount above the dome, the machinery humming like a living thing.

As she recalibrated the array, she felt something odd—as if *she* wasn't adjusting the instrument, but the instrument was adjusting *through* her.

Kai moved behind her, hands loosely folded. Nilas came to her right side, close enough that she felt the warmth of his strong, protective presence, the steadiness of him. Not intrusive. Not distracting. Grounding, anchoring her in a moment she sensed she could easily be swept out of. "Window opening in sixty seconds," Monika said, though her voice sounded distant even to herself.

The screens flickered. An unmistakable gentle hum vibrated up from the floor.

Nilas tensed. "Is that… inside the building?"

Kai answered, "It is inside the *field*."

Monika felt her pulse fall into rhythm with the hum, as if her body were an instrument being finely tuned. Her breath steadied. Her thoughts quieted. Her awareness expanded. "Thirty seconds," she whispered.

The night outside the glass wall shimmered, not visibly, but the way the air changes just before lightning splits a storm.

Nilas gripped the side of her console. "Monika… something's happening."

"Yes," Kai said softly. "Recognition."

The hum deepened. Monika's vision sharpened, crystalline, almost too clear. "Ten seconds." The harmonic line on her monitor elongated—not as static or data, but as a luminous golden thread.

Nilas inhaled sharply. "That isn't natural."

"No," Kai whispered. "It is intentional."

The countdown ended.

The golden window opened. The screens burst into a soft, amber radiance, not harsh, not blinding, but warm and ancient, as if an old memory had risen into the present moment.

The object appeared in startling clarity. Monika gasped, not in fear, but awe. A fissure along its black crystalline surface glowed with molten gold vapor. But the vapor didn't drift randomly; it curled and unfurled in perfect arcs, spirals, and loops, each movement deliberate, like sacred choreography.

Nilas whispered, "It's… beautiful."

Monika leaned forward, her heartbeat echoing in her ears. "It's symmetrical."

Kai shook his head slowly. "It is more than symmetrical. It is deliberate."

The vapor streams changed shape—aligning themselves into a curved lattice. A geometry she recognized instantly. "Nilas…" Her voice trembled. "It's forming the Universal Arc."

Kai nodded. "It is showing you what it remembers."

Nilas's brow furrowed. "But why show *us*?"

Kai answered simply. "Because humanity must see this."

A ring of golden vapor formed around the fissure.
A bloom of energy radiated outward.
Not like an explosion, but like a flower unfolding in slow, silent grace.

Monika whispered the truth. "It's a signature."

Nilas looked at her. "A signature of what?"

Kai placed his hand lightly on her shoulder, his touch steady and knowing. "Of origin."

The lattice expanded and Monika felt the pulse within her chest catch and sync with it.

Nilas's eyes widened. "Monika… your heartbeat, it's matching the rhythm."

She didn't answer. She didn't need to.

Her pulse no longer belonged to her alone.
It moved in perfect tandem with the golden wave inside the fissure, like two heartbeats merging across impossible distance.

Kai whispered, "You are attuning."

Nilas's voice shook. "Is she in danger?"

Kai shook his head. "No. She's awakening."

A final pulse flared, bright, gentle, breathtaking. Then the golden window closed. The screens dimmed. The humming faded. The mountain exhaled.

Nilas reached for Monika's hand, gripping it instinctively. She did not pull away. Her voice was a thin whisper. "It was alive."

Nilas swallowed. "The object?"

She nodded. "And it knew I was here."

Kai stepped forward, his presence wrapping around them like a quiet cloak. "This is the first window," he said softly. "Only the first."

Nilas turned to him. "What happens next?"

Kai's eyes warmed with truth. "The second window," he said, "opens the heart."

Caught At The Edge

CHAPTER SIX
Alignment Begins

The next morning felt unreal, as if the night had peeled away something thin and invisible between the world and the truth. The mountain was quiet. Too quiet. Not empty, not abandoned, but expectant.

Monika barely slept. Nilas didn't sleep at all. Kai never seemed to require sleep in the first place.

The three of them gathered in the observatory's viewing chamber as first light crept over the jagged volcanic ridges. Pale gold brushed across the horizon, softening the stone and casting long shadows across the floor. The *sunrise array* whirred softly through its morning calibration, bathing the room in muted blue and orange pulses that reflected off the metallic consoles and the glassed-in observation wall.

Nilas stood near the center of the room, his arms loosely crossed, posture relaxed but alert. He looked like he had carried the night on his shoulders; eyes tired yet bright, breath steady, mind working silently behind his calm exterior. He watched Monika with quiet intensity, waiting for her to place her hands back onto the console. Waiting to see what would happen when she did. The moment she lifted her fingers toward the controls, he felt it. *Sensed it.*

Something in her had changed. Not physically. Her face was the same attractive, determined, sharp-featured brilliance he'd seen since the day he met her. But internally, something had expanded. Something unhidden and awake. He held her gaze when she glanced at him, and there was something new in her eyes—a deeper calm, a deeper knowing, a deeper alignment. "You're quieter this morning," he said.

She didn't look up from her console. "I'm thinking."

"You're always thinking."

She paused—then allowed a faint, reluctant smile. "I guess I am."

Kai approached with silent steps, as if he moved inside a different layer of reality. His presence warmed the space, not physically, but energetically settling, grounding, clarifying. He stood beside her with the ease of someone who had always known exactly where to be.

"The first window always awakens the inner lens," he said gently.

Nilas turned toward him. "Inner lens?"

Monika stiffened almost imperceptibly, but she didn't turn away. "It's the part of consciousness that perceives energy," she said quietly. "Not just data. Intention."

Nilas let the words sink in. "You're saying the object opened something in you?"

Kai answered before she could.

"No. It recognized what was already there."

The words hit Monika in the chest as a truth her soul understood before her mind allowed it. She drew in a slow breath and shifted the telescope's orientation toward the object's predicted location. The screen lit with its faint signature; still small, still distant, but alive. She felt the resonance under her ribs, vibrating in the place where intuition meets memory.

Nilas stepped closer, unable to hide his concern and awe. "Monika… what happened? Last night wasn't normal."

"I know."

"You connected with it."

She froze for a heartbeat. She didn't deny it.

Kai moved between them, his voice soft and ancient. "Connection is not the danger. It is alignment."

Nilas turned to him sharply. "Alignment with *what*?"

Kai's eyes softened. "With the frequency the object carries. The same frequency that will sweep across the world when the final window opens."

Nilas exhaled slowly. "The reset."

Kai nodded once.

Monika swallowed hard, her hand trembling over the controls. "But why me?"

Kai regarded her with a depth she could barely stand to meet. "Because resonance follows recognition. Because you saw it before you *saw* it."

Nilas looked confused. "Meaning...?"

Monika answered quietly. "Meaning... its geometry was familiar to me in the vision. Before it appeared on the screens."

Kai nodded. "Exactly."

Nilas let out a breath he didn't realize he'd been holding. "So... what does that make her?"

Kai smiled gently. "Attuned."

Monika's pulse quickened. "To what degree?"

Kai stepped closer and hovered two fingers over the center of her sternum—not touching, just sensing. "To a degree that has not existed on Earth in many generations."

A shiver crawled up Nilas's spine. "That sounds... significant."

"It is more than significant," Kai said. "She is becoming a lens."

Monika stared at him. "A lens for what?"

"The second window."

The air in the room thickened, not with fear but with a gravity that pulled the soul deeper into itself. Monika clutched the edge of the console. "You mean when the object turns its fissure toward Earth?"

Kai nodded. "Yes."

Nilas stepped forward, voice tense. "How do we know it's going to turn?"

Kai turned to him, calm and sure. "Because it has already begun."

Monika snapped her attention to the rotational data. Her breath caught. The numbers had shifted. The object's rotational axis was tilting, slowly, deliberately, impossibly.

"It's reorienting," Nilas whispered.

Kai nodded. "Preparing."

"For what?" Nilas whispered.

"For proximity. For communication. For resonance with human consciousness."

Monika leaned in, heart pounding. "I can feel it. It's... expecting something."

"Yes," Kai said. "It is expecting alignment."

Nilas turned fully toward her, voice low and reverent. "And you're the first one aligning with it."

A long, thick silence filled the room. The object pulsed on the screen—and Monika's heartbeat echoed it perfectly. "It feels like it's breathing with me," she whispered.

Nilas stared at her, something shifting in his expression— awe, fear, recognition,
and something deeper he could not yet name.

Kai clasped his hands behind his back. "This is the beginning of attunement. First comes resonance. Then comes recognition. And then…" He hesitated.

Monika looked up sharply. "Then what?"

Kai held her gaze with an intensity that reverberated through the room. "Then comes remembrance."

The object pulsed again. The screen glowed softly. Monika's breath aligned with the rhythm, and she knew—Alignment had already begun.

Caught At The Edge

CHAPTER SEVEN
The First Witness

By the seventh day, the anomaly had stopped behaving like a statistical outlier. It behaved like a system. Across observatories, analysts began noticing the same thing — not through alerts or alarms, but through unease. The object's trajectory refused to degrade under scrutiny. Every correction applied to account for gravitational influence, solar pressure, or observational bias should have introduced variance. Instead, the opposite occurred. The more the data was stressed, the more coherent the path became.

At Mauna Kea, Dr. Reza Karimi had rerun the projection so many times he could see it when he closed his eyes. He leaned forward in his chair, elbows braced on the console, watching the vector hold steady through another refresh. "That's not passive motion," he said quietly. No one challenged him.

His assistant checked the timestamps again. "It's compensating before the deviation occurs."

Reza nodded. "Which means it's predicting the environment."

He didn't say the next thought out loud. Nothing predicts without intention.

Monika felt the shift in a different way. She had been tracking the object continuously since its discovery, reviewing the same datasets as everyone else, but something had changed overnight. The low hum beneath her sternum, the one she had learned to associate with true pattern emergence, had deepened. Not intensified. Stabilized. That unsettled her more.

She leaned back from the console and closed her eyes, allowing memory to surface. Not images. Geometry. The way certain trajectories *felt* when they were purposeful. The way coherent systems conserved motion instead of wasting it.

When she opened her eyes again, she bypassed the raw numbers and studied the path itself. The curve inward was restrained. Efficient. Anticipatory. No excess correction. No reactive drift.

This was not an object responding to forces. It was navigating them.

Hours later, standing with Nilas and Kai in the observatory, the same realization surfaced again, this time reinforced by instrumentation. Nilas gestured at the main display. "We're seeing the same thing everywhere. No drift, no tumble, no chaotic perturbation."

Monika nodded. "Because it's not entering along the ecliptic."

Nilas paused. "What?"

She adjusted the reference plane, rotating the model until the familiar flatness of the solar system tilted beneath the trajectory. "It's coming in above the planetary plane," she said. "North of the ecliptic."

Nilas straightened. "That rules out most known inbound debris."

"It rules out all of it," Monika replied.

She pulled up the back-projection and extended the vector outward; past the gas giants, past the Kuiper Belt, past the expected noise of near-field space. The line narrowed. It didn't fragment. It didn't diffuse. It converged.

An encrypted notification arrived moments later, flagged international priority. The data originated from Chile, where long-baseline instruments had independently confirmed the anomaly's coherence and back-traced its origin. The message was brief and formal: the object had been verified, its trajectory logged, and preliminary focus redirected toward the Sagittarius sector of the galaxy. Hawaii was instructed to assume primary observation.

Reza read the notice once, then again, before quietly saying, "This is no longer speculative."

Nilas exhaled slowly. "That doesn't stay local."

"No," Monika said. "And it doesn't wander." She brought up the galactic overlay. The projection shifted again, stars thickening as the trajectory pierced the plane of the Milky Way at a steep angle. The background radiation density increased sharply. The region was unmistakable to anyone trained to read stellar maps. Inner Milky Way. High-energy zone. Dense stellar population.

Kai had been silent until now. "Sagittarius," he said. The word landed with weight. Not symbolic, not dramatic, but definitive.

Nilas frowned. "The Sagittarius sector? Near the galactic center?"

"Yes," Monika said. "And that's not a place objects drift out of by chance."

Silence settled over the room as the implication took shape. An object originating from a region of that density, entering the solar system above the galactic plane, maintaining trajectory coherence across multiple gravitational regimes. This was not noise.

Across the globe, similar conclusions were forming independently. A radio astronomer in Chile flagged the same back-trace and quietly requested an independent review. A defense analyst in Alaska noted the anomalous entry angle and escalated it without knowing why. A mathematician in Reykjavík found herself unable to reconcile the stability curve with any known natural model. The awareness did not spread from a single source. It converged.

Reza broke it. "Chile logged it this morning," he said. "They've designated it **3I/ATLAS**."

Back in the observatory, Nilas rubbed his temples. "If this becomes public, people are going to ask why it's coming from that location."

"They'll ask what it wants," Monika said.

"And that question destabilizes systems," Kai added.

Nilas looked back at the display as the object corrected its course again; fractional, precise, anticipatory. "So, what are we dealing with?" he asked.

Kai answered without hesitation. "A catalyst." The word carried no comfort. Only inevitability.

Monika felt the pattern lock into place. The Universal Arc, the trajectory, the timing, the quiet global convergence of awareness. This wasn't an approach anymore. It was engagement.

And somewhere beyond the visible sky, an object that had begun its journey in the Sagittarius area of Earth's galaxy reaches of space, continued its deliberate descent, guided, intentional, now impossible to ignore.

This was the first moment when enough credible observers, working independently, saw the same impossible thing and did not dismiss it.

CHAPTER EIGHT
The Second Golden Window

Before it could be measured, it was felt. Something in the world's underlying rhythm had shifted so subtly that it escaped instruments at first, yet steadily enough that attention itself began to respond. Sleep patterns changed. Dreams sharpened. The space between moments seemed to tighten, as though awareness had less room to drift. It was not a sound, but a coherence.

Across the planet, responses appeared without agreement or explanation. Some felt an unnamable calm beneath rising uncertainty. Others sensed a pressure building, not as threat, but as insistence, an invitation to notice.

Animals reacted first. Migration paths bent. Calls altered pitch. Creatures paused where they had never paused before, alert to something beyond stimulus. No signal had been sent. No message received. Yet the field itself had begun to answer.

Time had not changed, but the space within it had. Then the second golden window approached, confirming it. That rising, insistent hum beneath Monika's sternum, the same place where every resonance had begun. But this time it wasn't gentle. It pressed inward, as though the object were leaning closer, demanding deeper attention, deeper memory. She arrived at the observatory early, long before sunset.

The moment she stepped into the room, she felt it the subtle charge in the air that curled around her skin like static. Her short blond hair, neatly styled to frame her striking features, lifted slightly with the electric tension of the night. Her posture was immaculate, clothes crisp and intentional, yet beneath the polished exterior her pulse throbbed with anticipation.

Nilas was already there. He sat cross-legged on the floor beside the main console; journal open in his lap. His tall frame was folded neatly, shoulders relaxed, yet his deep blue eyes were sharp. He was studying his notes with the focus of a man reading a prophecy.

He looked up the instant she entered. The concern in his expression was subtle but unmistakable. "It's stronger today," he said.

Monika didn't ask how he knew. His intuition had sharpened ever since the first window. "Yes," she murmured.

Kai stood near the large windows at the far end of the room, watching the horizon. His dark Polynesian features were calm, carved in serene lines, but the air around him trembled—not from fear, but from recognition. He turned to her as she approached. "The second window will open tonight," he said.

Monika set her bag down, her movements precise, disciplined. "What time?"

"Twenty-three minutes after midnight."

Nilas blinked. "Why that exact time?"

Kai didn't hesitate. "Because the Earth will cross the next resonance line then."

Nilas frowned, lowering his journal. "A resonance line? I've never heard of that."

"You wouldn't have," Kai said, "Science has not discovered them yet."

Monika stiffened. Not because she doubted him, but because she no longer fully trusted the models she had once lived by.

Gravity equations were bending under the object's influence. Harmonic frequencies defying known mathematics. Energy readings implying that space itself was elastic, responsive. Human understanding was too small for what was unfolding. The universe was larger. Older. More alive.

She turned to the console, fingers steady as she pulled up the latest rotational data. She froze instantly.

Nilas rose suddenly, crossing the room with long strides. "What is it?"

Monika pointed at the rotational axis.
"It's shifting again."

Kai approached with soft, certain steps. "The fissure is preparing to open."

Nilas felt his stomach drop. "Open toward what?"

Kai met his eyes. "Toward Earth."
A cold silence spread across the room.
Monika whispered, "The fissure is turning toward us."

Nilas swallowed. "Why?"

"Because it wants you to see," Kai said. "To understand."

Monika's pulse quickened. "Understand what?"

Kai's answer was simple and devastating. "That your laws of physics are incomplete."

Nilas whispered, "Incomplete how?"

Kai moved closer to the screen, raising a hand to the glass, not touching it, but feeling the resonance thrumming behind it. "Your world learned to measure matter," he said softly. "It never learned to measure intention."

The words sank into Monika's chest like a stone. Truth.

Nilas stared at the cascading energy, patterns. "Is this… intention?"

Kai nodded. "Yes. The object is forming a bridge. A deliberate harmonic. A pathway of coherence."

Monika leaned in, her strong features tightening with focus. She noticed it instantly; the fissure's light had changed.

They were no longer pale gold but now a deep, vivid copper. She whispered, "Copper-spectral gases."

Nilas frowned. "What does that mean?"

Her voice trembled. "It means the chemistry is changing again."

Kai added gently, "And the vibration with it."

Nilas exhaled slowly. "So… this is how it communicates."

"No," Kai corrected. "This is how it prepares you to understand." The screens flickered. The harmonic line rose sharply, one jagged spike, then a second, then a third. Not random. Not chaotic. A sequence.

Monika felt her chest tighten. "It's forming a pattern."

Nilas leaned closer beside her, breath shallow. "Is it trying to show us something?"

"Yes," she whispered. "But this isn't just a pattern. It's a language."

Kai nodded. "A language your world once knew, long before science replaced memory."

Nilas's voice dropped. "~~So~~ So, this object… it's rewriting more than physics."

"It is rewriting perception," Kai said.

Monika stared as the harmonic sequence stabilized—an arc within an arc, mirroring itself in exquisite symmetry.

Her hand lifted to her throat. "The Arc," she whispered.

Nilas turned sharply. "The Universal Arc?"

She nodded. "It's the same geometry."

Kai's voice carried a quiet reverence. "The object is revealing its origin."

The fissure pulsed, once, twice, then released a faint curl of copper-colored vapor that spiraled with deliberate grace.

Monika's breath hitched. "It's beautiful."

"It's precise," Kai said. "And precise beauty is never accidental."

Nilas whispered, "So what does the second window show us?"

Kai looked at him steadily. "It shows you what your science cannot yet remember."

The hum beneath Monika's sternum rose—warming, synchronizing with the copper light. Her voice emerged as a breath. "It's rewriting everything."

Kai placed a steady hand on her shoulder.
"No," he said softly. "It is awakening everything."
The fissure brightened
deeper, more resonant. The second golden window had begun to open. It was then the world had crossed from observation into engagement.

CHAPTER NINE
The Awakening of Nilas

Nilas had always believed himself to be an observer. A chronicler. An archivist. Someone who recorded the discoveries of others, never assuming he played any direct role in them. He never sought the spotlight. Never imagined himself woven into the greater puzzle. He stood tall in any room, but somehow always remained in the background, comfortable in silence. His ink-stained fingers and deep blue eyes captured the world rather than shaped it. But the night after the second golden window *changed something in him.*

He woke before dawn, breath sharp, heart racing, not from fear, but from *clarity.* His dreams had been filled with geometry; arcs, spirals, lattices of light folding and unfolding like breathing constellations. The movement was so precise, so familiar, that he wasn't sure the visions came from his own mind at all.

When he entered the observatory, Monika and Kai both turned toward him at the exact same moment, as if they *felt* him arrive, felt the shift moving through him. Monika studied him with her hazel eyes and sharp blond features softened by awe and concern. "You look... awake," she said.

Kai added, his voice warm and knowing, "Because he is."

Nilas paused in the doorway, the early light outlining the broad silhouette of his frame. "Awake how?" he asked quietly.

Kai stepped closer, his dark eyes and calm Polynesian presence radiating a steadying force. "You felt the sequence last night."

Nilas hesitated, then nodded slowly. "Yes. I don't know how. I don't know if it was a dream or—"

"It was not a dream," Kai said softly. "It was contact."

Nilas's breath caught.

Monika moved toward him, her posture compact, clothes neat and immaculate, short blond hair framing her strong features as she studied him closely.

"Nilas… you didn't tell me you were feeling it."

"I didn't know how to say it," he admitted, rubbing the back of his neck.

Kai gave a gentle, almost fatherly smile. "You do not need to explain something the mind is not designed to hold."

Nilas sank into the nearest chair, his tall frame folding forward as though the weight of the truth had finally settled onto him.

"So…this is real," he murmured. "What's happening to me."

Monika sat beside him, her presence grounding. "I think it started when you were helping me through the resonance. You touched my arm, and…"

"And your energetic fields brushed," Kai finished. "Energy awakens through proximity. Through recognition. Through alignment."

Nilas exhaled slowly. "So… I'm aligning too?"

Kai nodded. "Yes. Your alignment takes a different form."

Monika tilted her head, curious. "How?"

Kai turned to her, speaking softly but with the gravity of truth. "Nilas is a recorder.
Not just on paper. In consciousness."

Nilas blinked, deep blue eyes widening. "A recorder?"

Kai nodded, pleased. "There are souls," he said, "who have lived many lifetimes observing the unfolding of ages. Not as leaders, not as visionaries, but as *witnesses*. Carriers of memory when worlds change."

Nilas stared at him, stunned. "You think I'm one of those?"

Kai's voice softened into reverence. "You are."

Monika placed her hand on Nilas's forearm, her touch steady. "It makes sense," she said quietly. "You always know what matters.
You always feel the moment before it happens."

Nilas swallowed, overwhelmed. His heartbeat in a tight, trembling rhythm. "It still doesn't explain the dreams."

Kai stepped closer. "Your dreams are not dreams," he said gently. "They are recall. Fragments of memory returning."

Nilas stiffened. "Memory of what?"

Kai met his eyes. "Of whom you were before this life."

Silence pooled between them. Alive. Heavy. Sacred.

Nilas whispered, "What did I remember?"

Kai's voice was calm, ancient. "You remembered the Arc."

Monika inhaled sharply.

Nilas whispered again, barely audible, "The Universal Arc?"

Kai nodded. "Yes. You recognized its geometry before your mind even learned the words. That is why you felt the second window. That is why the object touched you."

Nilas leaned back, breath unsteady. "Why me, then?"

Kai stepped in front of him and held two fingers lightly above Nilas's heart, not touching, but aligning, sensing.

"Because your soul carries the record of these cycles. You are not new to this. You have seen worlds awaken before."

Nilas felt something vibrate through his ribs, his chest, his spine, like truth moving back into place.

Monika watched him, her own resonance humming in sympathy.

"And Monika?" Nilas asked softly, turning to her.

Kai smiled.

"She was the one meant to hear the object."

"And you," Kai said, looking back at him, "were meant to remember it."

Nilas's throat tightened.

Monika whispered, "Nilas… this is why you're here."

His eyes softened, full of questions and a dawning understanding.

"So that's why I felt the fissure? Why the patterns looked familiar?"

Kai nodded. "Yes. Your soul recognized the harmonic language." He added quietly: "And soon, others will too."

Nilas leaned forward, elbows on his knees, head in his hands.

"This is… bigger than anything I've ever imagined."

Monika's voice was a breath. "It's bigger than all of us."

Kai folded his hands behind his back. "And it is only the beginning."

Nilas turned toward the eastern windows, where the first pale hues of dawn brushed the sky with rose and silver. He felt something stir in his chest; a pulse, a memory, a belonging that was older than this lifetime. He whispered to the stillness, as though answering a call across centuries, "I think I remember."

Monika smiled softly. Kai nodded, eyes warm. Somewhere in the darkness of space, *the object pulsed back*, soft, rhythmic, echoing his awakening with a resonance all its own.

Monika noticed it first in her body, not on the instruments.

It was not fear. Not urgency. It was the sudden sensation that something which had always been present, something assumed, like pressure or background light, had quietly withdrawn. The room felt fractionally larger, as though an invisible tension had been released. She paused, one hand resting on the edge of the console, listening inwardly before looking outward.

The displays were steady. Signal strength nominal. Time stamps aligned. Nothing registered as wrong. Yet her sense of timing felt subtly displaced, as if the moment she was standing in had slipped a half-step ahead of itself. Cause and effect no longer arrived together. The world felt briefly asynchronous.

She closed her eyes.

What came was not an image but an impression: a lattice loosening. Not breaking, but unhooking. Something had disengaged from a larger pattern, not violently, not in protest, but with precision. As if it had completed a function and moved on. She had the unsettling sense that whatever had shifted was no longer participating in the same field of reference.

Monika straightened and opened her eyes. She scanned the room again, slower this time, as if expecting the space itself to respond. Nothing did. The observatory remained calm, obedient, blind.

She considered recording the sensation. Her fingers hovered over the input panel. There was no language for what she had felt, no category that would not immediately invite correction or dismissal. After a moment, she entered a single line into the log, deliberately neutral, almost banal, and closed the file.

The feeling passed, but the silence it left behind did not. Whatever had shifted was already beyond the reach of instruments.

Caught At The Edge

CHAPTER TEN
The World Pauses

The first anomaly was so minor it barely warranted comment. A transmission had arrived out of sequence, delayed by a margin small enough to be blamed on calibration drift. A routine relay required a second request. Someone joked about solar noise. The systems adjusted and moved on.

Monika said nothing. As she watched the data settle back into place, the earlier sensation returned, not as intensity, but as recognition. The absence she had felt was not empty. It was *elsewhere*. Whatever had stepped out of alignment had done so cleanly, leaving no debris behind, no evidence of passage.

Around her, the world continued as if uninterrupted. Schedules held. Conversations resumed. Explanations queued themselves automatically.

Monika understood, with a quiet certainty that did not need confirmation, that the moment of separation had already occurred and that what followed would not announce itself all at once.

Some events, she knew, are only visible in retrospect.

The world did not change all at once. It shifted quietly. A softness spread across humanity, subtle enough to be ignored by the distracted, unmistakable to the sensitive. People awoke that morning with a strange sense of calm, as though a long-held tension had dissolved in their sleep. Arguments faded before they began. Old resentments loosened their grip. Even the air felt different, lighter, clearer, as if the planet itself had exhaled.

Monika sensed it instantly. When she stepped outside before dawn, the stillness was profound, almost sacred. The wind held its breath. Birds perched silently along the telephone wires. The mountains stood unmoving, as though honoring a moment older than time.

Nilas joined her outside the observatory, mug of tea warming both hands, his light brown hair wind-tossed, his deep blue eyes thoughtful. "You feel it too," he said softly.

Monika nodded. "Yes."

"What is it?"

She looked toward the horizon, watching the faint edge of gold appear behind the mountains. "A lull," she said. "The universe is holding still."

Nilas shivered, though the air was mild. "It feels like the world is waiting."

Kai stepped through the doorway behind them, framed by the rising light, his dark Polynesian features serene, his presence carrying the same calm that had settled across the planet. "It is," he said.

They turned toward him. Kai stepped closer. "This is the pause before remembrance."

Inside, the observatory felt suspended; machines humming, monitors glowing, yet everything wrapped in a delicate stillness, like a breath held between heartbeats.

Monika returned to the console. The object pulsed on the screen, faint, steady, rhythmic, like a heartbeat echoing from across the solar system.

Nilas moved to her side. "Has the resonance changed?"

"No," she said softly. "The resonance hasn't changed. We have."

Nilas studied her expression. "What do you mean?"

Monika's fingers hovered over the controls. "Before, it was noise mixed with pattern. Today it's clearer. Like it's easier to hear."

Kai nodded behind them. "The object's transmission has not shifted. Human consciousness has."

Nilas frowned. "All of humanity?"

"No," Kai replied quietly. "But enough."

Monika felt the truth of that in her chest, a soft hum just beneath the sternum.

Nilas leaned closer, lowering his voice. "Is this what you meant by summoning?"

"Yes," Kai said. "Humanity is beginning to turn inward. To remember its own resonance."

Nilas exhaled slowly. "I've never felt anything like this."

"You have," Kai said gently. "But not in this lifetime."

Nilas blinked, unsettled but not afraid.

Monika reached over, her short blonde hair brushing her cheek, and lightly touched his wrist. "Kai's right. This calm… it feels old. Familiar."

Nilas nodded slowly. "Like a memory I can't quite place."

"Exactly," she whispered.

A soft chime murmured. The screen flickered. Nilas inhaled sharply. "Is that—?"

Monika zoomed in. The object had slowed. Not dramatically—just enough to feel it, like sensing a shift in a rhythm you've begun to understand.

Kai stepped forward. "It is entering proximity."

Nilas stiffened. "Proximity to what?"

"To consciousness," Kai said calmly.

Monika turned from the screen, stunned. "You mean to *us*."

Kai nodded. "Yes."

Nilas's heartbeat quickened. "But it's still millions of miles away."

"Distance does not separate fields," Kai said softly. "Only perception does."

Monika felt that inner hum rising again, warm and insistent.

Nilas touched a hand to his own chest, startled. "I… I feel something too."

Kai closed his eyes for a moment, then opened them with a slow exhale.

"The world is feeling it. People will describe it differently—peace, clarity, unease, stillness. But they will all know something is happening."

Monika whispered, "It's awakening them."

Kai inclined his head. "Yes."

Nilas stared at the faint pulse on the screen. "What happens when everyone wakes up?"

Kai answered without hesitation. "They see truth."

Nilas swallowed. "What truth?"

Kai approached the display, his voice quiet and steady. "That they were never separate. That consciousness is universal. That memory is older than the mind. And that the universe is alive."

A long, heavy silence settled.

Monika typed slowly, almost unconsciously, her fingers moving as though guided from within. "Nilas," she said softly, "your dreams… are they clearer today?"

He swallowed hard. "Yes. Very."

"What did you see?"

He hesitated, then answered in a trembling whisper.

"An arc. Not the Universal Arc in the sky… but something larger. A movement. A… curvature of energy."

Monika felt her breath catch. "That's not just a dream."

Kai nodded. "He is remembering his part."

Nilas looked shaken. "My part in what?"

"The awakening," Kai said.

Nilas fell silent.

Monika felt a deep tenderness rise in her, a recognition, a knowing. She reached out and placed her hand over his.

He didn't pull away. The monitor pulsed again, soft and golden.

Kai whispered, "The world is pausing so it can take its first conscious breath."

Monika stared at the screen. "It's waiting for us."

Nilas whispered, "Waiting for what?"

Kai's voice carried the weight of ancient certainty. "For the moment we begin to see."

CHAPTER ELEVEN
The First Departures

No one expected the first departures. Not the governments, not the scientists, not the world glued to its screens. The departure wave did not begin with panic or chaos. It did not begin with illness, disaster, or fear. It began with peace. A kind of peace humanity had forgotten.

In every country, across every time zone, people who had carried long suffering—elders, the exhausted, the ones whose bodies had been weary for years, began to slip quietly from this world.

Not violently. Not tragically. But gently, as though something had touched their souls and whispered, *You may rest now.*

Monika saw the reports first. She sat at the observatory console, her short blonde hair catching faint glints of the dawn light, her neatly pressed shirt immaculate even after a sleepless night. Her posture, straight, controlled, composed, contrasted the tremor in her hands as she scrolled through the global data feeds, unable to make sense of what she was reading.

The numbers rose steadily, evenly—like a tide coming in. The cause of death repeated the same phrase: *peaceful natural passing.*

Nilas stood behind her, tall and quiet, his light brown hair mussed from hours of running his hands through it, deep blue eyes scanning the screens over her shoulder. He exhaled sharply, breath tightening. "What is this?" he murmured. "A global event?"

Monika's voice was a whisper. "It's all synchronized."

Before either could speak again, Kai entered the room. He 5' 7" frame moved like a soft current; fluid, grounded, dark hair falling softly around his Polynesian features. His deep brown eyes absorbing more than the screens could reveal. He paused only a moment, his expression neither surprised nor alarmed. Only solemn. Only reverent. "It has begun," he said.

Nilas turned to him. "What has begun?"

Kai stepped forward, hands folding behind his back in the graceful way he often stood when speaking truth. "The first wave of crossings."

Monika's chest tightened. "Crossings… like death?"

"Yes," Kai said gently. "Not as your world understands it—sadly, for those left behind."

Nilas swallowed. "Then how?"

Kai walked toward the large window overlooking the mountains. The morning light poured across the snow with an almost unreal softness, turning the peaks into shimmering gold.

"When a world awakens," he said softly, "many souls choose to complete their life contracts. They have done their work. They have held the light through the darkest cycles. They stay until the moment the frequency begins to shift… and then they go home."

Monika stared at the global reports, her neat composure cracking at the edges. "So… they're not dying."

"No," Kai said. "They are being released."

Nilas whispered, "Released from what?"

"From the gravity of incarnation. From pain. From burden. From exhaustion."

Monika's throat tightened, an ache that wasn't sadness, but deep recognition.

"These are the old souls," she murmured. "The ones who carried humanity through its darkest eras."

Kai nodded. "Yes."

Nilas rubbed the back of his neck, pacing a short line across the room.

"If this continues, people will panic. They'll think something is wrong."

"Something *is* happening," Kai replied. "But nothing is wrong."

Monika's voice steadied. "Why now?"

"Because the second golden window opened their departure path."

Kai's tone softened into something nearly sacred. "Because they cannot ascend into the new frequency while bound to the old."

Nilas turned, stunned. "Is this connected to the object?"

Kai's answer was immediate. "Everything is connected to the object."

Monika felt her breath catch. "Then what activated this wave?"

Kai stepped close to her console, placing a hand near, but not touching the harmonic display. "When the second window opened, the object's resonance touched the soul-field of the Earth. Those who were ready recognized the call."

Nilas lowered himself into a chair, overwhelmed. "They wanted to leave?"

"They wanted to complete," Kai corrected.

Monika wiped a tear from her cheek, a rare crack in her poised exterior. "It's beautiful," she whispered. "And heartbreaking."

Kai nodded. "Great changes often begin with great mercy."

The room fell into silence. They watched the global data quietly. There were thousands of lights extinguishing not in fear, not in violence, but in gentle release.

Then Monika gasped.

The object pulsed on the screen. A soft, golden flicker, and the harmonic field around the observatory warmed, humming faintly in the center. "It's happening again," she whispered.

Nilas leaned in. "What does it mean?"

Kai closed his eyes for a long, still moment. "It means," he said softly, "the object has acknowledged the first wave."

Monika felt her chest ache, this time with reverence, not fear. "It's honoring them," she whispered.

"Yes," Kai murmured. "It is."

Nilas shut his eyes, fighting the emotion rising in his throat. "This… changes everything."

Kai nodded. "It does. Because now humanity will feel the shift not just in the sky… but in their hearts."

Monika looked back to the monitor, the golden pulse glowing steadily.

"We're not losing them," she said softly. "They're being carried."

Kai's voice deepened into its rarest register—reverent, ancient, knowing. "They are becoming part of the song."

Nilas shut his eyes, holding back tears. "What happens next?"

Kai turned toward the horizon, where the morning light hovered without warmth or urgency. "There is always a pause," he said. "A breath."

Monika felt it then, not as information, but as sensation. The space between her thoughts widened. The ache in her chest softened into stillness.

The world did not feel broken. It felt rearranged.

Outside, nothing dramatic occurred. No alarms sounded. No skies darkened. Yet something subtle had shifted, like a great wheel turning beneath the surface of things. Humanity stood inside that turning; half in what had been, half in what had not yet arrived.

The world was not ending. It was turning. And the pause had begun.

Caught At The Edge

CHAPTER 12
The Prophecy Line

By the time the first wave of crossings settled, the world had begun to quiet in a way that felt almost unnatural. Traffic eased. Hospitals reported fewer emergencies. Even global conflicts simmered into pauses, like a collective exhale rising from the planet itself. The quiet was not peace. It was anticipation. It felt like a thin and luminous stillness, as if all of humanity were standing at the threshold of a door that had not yet opened.

Monika felt it more intensely than anyone. The hum beneath her sternum, once gentle, now pulsed with a steady rhythm; felt closer to a drumbeat than a whisper. Her hair framed the sharpness of her features, and even her immaculate composure could not hide the deeper tremor moving through her.

Nilas noticed it first. With deep blue eyes that missed nothing, he watched her with growing concern.

"You keep touching your chest," he said softly.

She dropped her hand, startled. "I didn't realize."

Before Nilas could respond, Karolin stepped into the room. She moved with quiet command, long blonde hair cascading over a moss-green sweater, Swedish bone structure giving her an ethereal beauty. Her presence always brought a grounded calmness. A smile touched her face, open and genuine, as though she was exactly where she wanted to be.

Nilas turned toward her, relief flickering through him. "This is my sister, Karolin," he said, looking from her to Monika and Kai. "She flew in from Sweden last night."

Karolin smiled at them both. "I'm really glad to finally meet you," she said warmly.

Monika returned the smile, studying her with quiet curiosity. Kai nodded in acknowledgment, his expression attentive but receptive.

Karolin's gaze shifted back to Monika, her tone gentle, certain. "Your field is shifting. I could feel it from across the room."

Monika blinked, surprised but not unsettled. "You feel energies too?"

Karolin nodded. "I've felt resonance since childhood. I just didn't have a name for it."

Kai chimed in, the Polynesian calm in his dark eyes deepening at the sight of Karolin. "You sensed the arrival," he said gently.

Karolin met his gaze without flinching. "Yes. The same way I knew to come here."

Nilas exhaled. "She flew from Stockholm without knowing why."

Karolin offered a knowing smile. "I knew why. I just didn't understand it yet."

Kai turned toward Monika. "The object is preparing the next harmonic exchange," he said. "The third window is still ahead… but this—" he gestured to Monika's chest "—this is the Prophecy Line."

Monika's breath caught. "I felt something last night," she said. "Something sharp. Like a thread pulling through time."

Karolin stepped closer, instinctively grounding her with a touch to the arm, her hand strong, warm. "What did it feel like?" she asked.

"Structure," Monika whispered. "A sequence. A line of light."

Kai nodded. "Yes. She is describing the Prophecy Line."

Nilas looked between them, overwhelmed. "What does it mean?"

Kai activated the harmonic overlay. The screen brightened with the soft arc of golden vapor. "The Prophecy Line," he said, "is the moment when the object reveals its purpose."

Karolin drew closer, her eyes widening. "Is that... the Arc's geometry?"

Monika nodded. "It's the same curvature I saw in the vision."

Karolin whispered, "It feels like memory."

Nilas swallowed hard. "Memory of what?"

Kai answered, "Of the cycle before this one."

Karolin's breath hitched softly, a subtle sign Monika registered it instinctively.

She asked, "Do you remember something?"

Karolin placed a hand on her chest. "Not with my mind. But my body... yes. It recognizes this pattern."

Kai nodded approvingly. "Karolin has an open resonance-field. She is attuned to origin frequencies."

Nilas frowned. "Origin frequencies... meaning?"

Karolin answered for him, voice low. "Meaning I was born remembering a little more than most."

Monika felt a sudden clarity. "You're meant to help us."

Kai smiled softly. "She is meant to help *many*."

The harmonic arc brightened again, pulsing with intention.

"It's pointing at Earth," Monika whispered.

Karolin took a slow breath. "It's a pathway."

"A pathway to awakening," Kai said.

Karolin's eyes softened, a deep maternal compassion moving through her. "This will touch everyone. Not just the sensitive."

Nilas touched the screen lightly. "So…what does it say?"

Monika closed her eyes, letting the hum rise through her sternum. The message came through her — not as words, but as knowing: Prepare. The cycle is turning. Remember who you are. The new world approaches.

Karolin shuddered, tears welling. "I felt that. Every word."

Nilas looked at her in astonishment. "You did?"

Karolin nodded, wiping a tear. "It's the same frequency that guided me here."

Kai stepped closer, voice reverent. "She is aligned with the incoming resonance. When the Third Window opens, Karolin will help stabilize those who awaken early."

Nilas whispered, shaken, grateful: "You always were the strong one."

Karolin squeezed his hand. "And you always were the remembering one."

The screen pulsed again; bright, gold, seismic. Monika whispered
"It's coming."

Kai nodded. "The Prophecy Line is the last warning… and the first blessing."

Karolin stepped to Monika's side, standing with her shoulder-to-shoulder.

"And we," Karolin said softly, "are exactly where we need to be."

Caught At The Edge

CHAPTER 13

When the Souls Begin to Leave

No alarms sounded. No sirens warned the world. The second wave arrived quietly—so quietly that most people only noticed it after it had already passed through them.

The second wave did not arrive as gently as the first. The first had been peaceful, almost invisible—a release of those who had carried too much for too long. The second wave was different. It spread throughout the world like a low, resonant hum, awakening something deep in the hearts of those who remained.

People began feeling strange pulses in their chests, not fear, not pain, but a subtle loosening, like a knot untying itself after a lifetime of tension. Nurses reported that patients who had been restless suddenly became serene. Families sat at the bedsides of their loved ones and felt an inexplicable calm settle over the room.

Monika felt it in her bones. She sensed the wave before she read a single report, long before any alert pinged across the global networks. At dawn, while wind swept over the mountaintop and clouds drifted low across the valley, a soft ache blossomed beneath her sternum. Not sharp, not alarming, but deep and vast, like a door opening inside her chest. She touched her hand to her heart, breath catching.

Nilas walked into the observatory and saw her expression shift. His tall frame was tense, brown hair still tousled from sleep, his eyes dark with worry. *"You felt it."*

Monika nodded, unable to speak.

Karolin entered moments later, her long hair flowing down her shoulders, stunning even in simple clothes, her bright blue eyes flashing, her presence warm and steady. She paused in the doorway, sensing the energy the instant she crossed the threshold. "Something's moved in the field," she said softly. "I don't know what else to call it—an energy wave. That's how it feels to me."

Kai appeared behind them, silent, solemn, his Polynesian features calm and knowing, his presence shifting the air as if announcing the arrival of truth itself. "The second wave has begun."

Nilas's voice shook. "These people… they aren't suffering, are they?"

"No," Kai said. "They are surrendering."

Monika stared at him. "Surrendering to what?"

Kai lifted his gaze toward the sky. "To the call."

Monika stepped to her console, fingers trembling as she pulled up the global monitor. A slow stream of reports scrolled across the screen; deaths marked as peaceful, sudden, quiet. People lying down to rest and not waking up. Individuals simply exhaling and slipping into stillness.

Nilas's voice was almost inaudible. "It's increasing."

"Yes," Kai murmured. "Because the resonance is deepening."

Karolin moved behind Monika, placing a gentle hand on her shoulder, grounding her, steadying her. "Letthe energy wave move through you," she whispered. "Don't resist."

Monika wiped a tear from the corner of her eye. She didn't fully understand why she was crying. Grief, yes, but also something else. Something softer. Something luminous. "They're not leaving in fear."

"No," Kai agreed, "because they are not dying. They are being transitioned."

Nilas swallowed hard. "Transitioned into what?"

"Into memory," Kai said. "Into light."

The ache in Monika's chest deepened into warmth. "I can feel them," she whispered. "It's like they're rising."

"They are," Kai said. "They are crossing into a higher vibration field. They will be guided from there."

Nilas sank into a chair, overwhelmed. "Witnessing this is… unbelievable."

"It's natural," Kai said gently. "A world does not awaken alone."

Monika closed her eyes. "Why now? Why at this exact moment?"

Kai folded his hands behind him. "Because the Prophecy Line opened. Once it opened, the souls who agreed to shepherd the transition completed their work."

Nilas whispered, "So these people… they chose this?"

"Yes," Kai said. "Long before they incarnated. It was part of their soul contract."

Karolin nodded softly, eyes shimmering. "Old souls always leave first. They clear the way."

Monika felt her breath catch. "They're not victims."

"They are volunteers," Kai said.

Outside, the world was changing. Families gathered, not in terror, but in unity. People called loved ones they hadn't spoken to in years. Strangers comforted each other on street corners. Hospitals reported a phenomenon they could not explain. Heart rates slowing in perfect synchrony moments before crossing.

Nilas watched the data scroll, awestruck. "It's like the whole planet is breathing together."

"The second wave prepares humanity for the Third Window," Kai murmured.

Monika looked up sharply. "The Third Window... the one before the descent?"

"Yes," Kai said. "And before alignment becomes global."

Nilas's hands shook. "Monika... does this hurt you? Feeling all of this?"

She turned to him, eyes soft beneath her reshelved hair, her features sharp but vulnerable. "It doesn't hurt. It feels... familiar. Like I've been through a transition before."

Nilas exhaled shakily. "You're remembering."

Kai's voice grew quiet. "She is a lens and lenses feel everything first."

Karolin brushed a tear from her cheek, watching Monika with a mixture of admiration and sorrow. "You're holding the field for many."

Monika's heart ached again; a warm, swelling ache, and she understood, suddenly, what the second wave truly meant.

"It's love," she whispered. "They're not leaving because they're afraid. They're leaving because they're being lifted."

Nilas wiped tears from his eyes.

Kai nodded. "Yes. They are being lifted into the energetic field that will help stabilize the new world."

The harmonic pulse of the object changed again, softer now, more tender. Monika felt every departing soul as a flutter of light inside her chest.

Nilas reached out and took her hand without thinking, needing to anchor himself to someone he cared for and trusted; something solid, something alive.

She didn't pull away.

Kai watched them both, as though witnessing an ancient alignment reawakening between two soul-fields that had traveled lifetimes together.

"The second wave is mercy," he said softly.
"The third wave will be awakening."

Monika and Nilas exchanged a look, one filled with fear, wonder, and recognition. Karolin stepped closer, linking her presence into theirs — a triad forming without words.

The world was turning. The souls were beginning to rise.

Caught At The Edge

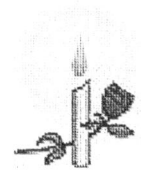

CHAPTER 14
The Third Golden Window

No one announced the Third Golden Window. It arrived because it had reached its moment. The night of the arrival fell upon the Earth with a weight that felt ancient—not heavy but destined.

The air over the mountaintop shimmered with an electric quiet, as if every molecule were listening. The clouds parted without wind. The sky deepened to a dark sapphire; too clear, too vast, too expectant.

Monika sensed it before she reached the observatory door. The hum beneath her sternum, once gentle, now insistent, tightened into a luminous thread running down her spine. Her breath trembled. Not from fear. From recognition.

Nilas met her at the entrance. His silhouette outlined by the glow of the hallway lights. His deep blue eyes softened when he saw her. "You feel it too."

Monika nodded. "It's close."

Karolin stepped forward from the shadows of the corridor, her hair glowing in the dim light, her presence carrying a stillness that matched the night. "The field is opening," she murmured. "I can feel it all the way down the mountain."

Kai was already inside, standing before the main screen, hands folded, posture still, expression solemn. The light from the monitors cast a faint halo around him. He turned as they entered. "The Third Window opens tonight."

Nilas swallowed. "At what time?"

Kai's voice lowered, as though speaking across centuries. "Midnight. Exact."

Monika's pulse jumped. "The exact midpoint between the Prophecy Line and the descent."

Kai nodded. "Yes."

Looking for comfort, Nilas moved closer to Monika. "What will this window show us?"

Kai looked at the screen, eyes glinting with a truth too large to fully hold. "The fissure," he said quietly, "will open."

They approached the central console.

Monika adjusted the instrument array. Her fingers shook slightly, though her mind felt sharper than ever, as if each harmonic the object had sent had tuned her deeper into clarity.

Nilas stood beside her, steady and anchored.

Karolin leaned against the glass wall nearby, arms crossed lightly, her intuitive senses already active, listening to something beyond sound.

Kai remained behind them, guardian and witness.

The minutes dissolved into silence. At 11:57 p.m., the harmonic signature began to rise. Slowly. Gracefully. Like light pushing through the cracks of an unseen doorway.

Monika felt the pulse in her sternum match it perfectly.

Nilas's breath hitched. "Monika… your heart rate…"

"I know," she whispered. "It's synchronizing."

Kai nodded. "As it was meant to."

Karolin closed her eyes, a shiver running through her. "It's touching the entire mountain."

11:59 p.m.

The monitors brightened. A faint arc of gold shimmered across the object's fissure.

Nilas whispered, "It's starting."

Monika leaned close, eyes wide. "The geometry... it's changing."

Kai took a step forward. "The object is aligning its inner core toward Earth."

Nilas stiffened. "Why now?"

"Because humanity has entered the threshold between the old frequency and the new," Kai said. "The Third Window bridges them."

Monika touched the screen lightly. "The fissure... it's widening."

A soft vibration filled the room—not from machinery, not from sound—but from space itself. The object pulsed. Once. Twice. Then a deep harmonic rose, trembling through Monika's bones.

Nilas's eyes widened. "Do you feel that?"

Monika nodded, unable to speak.

Kai answered for her, "Yes. She feels it first."

Karolin pressed a hand over her own heart. "I feel the outskirts of it… but Monika — it's going straight into you."

Midnight.

The Third Golden Window opened. The fissure expanded into a radiant plume of light—gold, rose, copper, sapphire, pale green, colors that existed but did not exist in human physics. Gas streamed outward in a precise, spiraling geometry.

Nilas whispered, breath trembling, "It's like a flower…"

Monika finished softly,"…opening toward us."

Kai's grew still. "This is the Revelation Spiral."

Monika's eyes filled. "It's beautiful."

Nilas couldn't look away. "It's intentional."

"Yes," Kai said. "The object is revealing its inner structure… its origin… its purpose."

Karolin stepped closer, her voice barely audible. "It's conscious."

Monika whispered, "Look."

At the heart of the fissure, a luminous arc curved downward — the exact curvature of the Universal Arc seen across the heavens on March 23, 2024.

Nilas gasped. "It's the same shape."

Monika trembled. "It's telling us it's connected."

Kai nodded slowly. "The Universal Arc was not a coincidence. It was the first signature of the cycle. The object carries the second."

The spiral widened again. Gas streamed outward like petals unfurling. Each color carried its own harmonic. Each harmonic its own intention. Each intention its own truth.

Karolin's eyes shimmered. "It's speaking in light."

Monika's voice cracked: "It's remembering us."

"No," Kai said gently. "It is helping you remember."

Nilas turned to him, fear and awe blending in his voice. "Remember what?"

Kai stepped forward. "That humanity is part of a larger truth. That consciousness is not confined to flesh. That awakening comes not through knowledge…but through recognition."

Monika closed her eyes as another pulse passed through her. "It feels like… home."

Nilas's throat tightened. "Monika…"

Kai nodded. "Yes. She is remembering the cycle."

Karolin wiped a tear from her cheek. "She knew she was born for this moment."

The fissure pulsed a final time. A long, low wave of golden resonance swept across the observatory, vibrating through the glass, through the walls, through their hearts.

The Third Window concluded. The screens dimmed back to their ordinary glow. Monika leaned against the console, breath shaking.

Nilas steadied her, hands warm around her arms. "Are you all right?"

She nodded slowly. "I saw something," she whispered. "Not vision… not memory… something in-between."

Kai's expression softened. "You saw the beginning of your remembrance."

Nilas looked between them. "So…what happens now?"

Kai answered with quiet gravity. "Now the object begins its turn toward Earth."

Monika swallowed. "And after that?"

Kai met her eyes. "The descent."

Nilas exhaled, shaken.

Karolin stepped beside Monika, offering silent support.

Monika whispered: "The world is about to change."

Kai nodded. "And so are you."

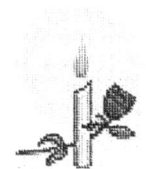

CHAPTER 15
The Night of the Turning

Night settled over the mountain like a veil drawn slowly across the world. Not heavy, not silent — but *expectant*. Monika felt it the moment the Sun dipped behind the peaks. A subtle tightening in the air. A slow rising of the hum beneath her sternum. A shifting in the gravity inside her bones. The Third Golden Window had passed. Now came the night of the turning.

Nilas waited for her outside the observatory, leaning against the railing, arms folded against the cold. When he saw her step into the dim light, he straightened instantly, sensing the weight she carried. "You feel it," he said quietly.

"Yes," Monika whispered. "It's beginning."

Kai appeared behind her, closing the door behind him. He nodded once, as though confirming an agreement made long ago. "The object will initiate its rotational turn within the hour."

Reza's console chimed sharply—different from the harmonic tones. Administrative. External. He glanced down, frowned, then looked up at Kai. "We've been pulled into a joint call," he said. "Europe initiated it. France is hosting."

Nilas stiffened. "Now?"

"Yes," Reza replied. "They're calling it an emergency coordination briefing."

Monika felt it immediately—not resonance, not intuition—but resistance. The kind that preceded confrontation.

The main screen shifted. Grids rearranged. Windows populated.

Three feeds locked in.

Paris.
Berlin.
Santiago.

Henri' appeared first. He sat upright in a glass-walled control room, posture rigid, expression sharp. Silver hair cut precisely. Dark eyes alert, unsmiling. He did not acknowledge anyone immediately—only scanned data streaming beside his image.

Frederick appeared a moment later, calm and immaculately composed, hands folded loosely on the table in front of him. He nodded once toward Reza.

Juan's feed flickered, then stabilized. He looked tired. Focused. "We're tracking it continuously now," he said without preamble. "Velocity increase confirmed. Rotational turn imminent."

Henri' cut in sharply. "That assessment is premature."

Juan didn't rise to it. "The numbers are stable."

Henri' turned slightly toward Frederick's window. "Germany is placing far too much confidence in extrapolation," he said coolly. "And far too much influence in uncredentialed analysis."

The word landed exactly where it was intended.

Monika kept her eyes on the screen.

Frederick did not. "Monika is here at my request," he said evenly. "And she stays."

Henri' exhaled through his nose. "This is not a metaphysical symposium," he snapped. "We are observing a physical object on a measurable descent trajectory."

Kai did not speak.

Reza leaned forward. "Henri', with respect, the Chilean data—"

"I am aware of the Chilean data," Henri' interrupted. "What I am not aware of is why Hawaii is allowing non-staff influence during a critical tracking phase."

Silence stretched.

Frederick's voice remained level. "Because the object is not behaving as debris, and you know it."

Henri's jaw tightened. "That does not give us license to abandon protocol."

Juan interjected quietly. "Protocol doesn't explain why it corrected course before our last gravitational adjustment."

Henri' turned back to his screens. "Then your model is incomplete."

"Yes," Frederick said. "It is."

That landed harder than argument.

Henri' looked up slowly. "You're suggesting intent."

"I'm suggesting acknowledgment," Frederick replied. "Those are not the same thing."

The room fell quiet.

On Monika's console, the harmonic line deepened—slower now, heavier. The turn was close.

Reza broke the silence. "Regardless of interpretation, the object is rotating."

Juan nodded. "Confirmed."

Henri' said nothing.

The data did not care.

Nilas inhaled sharply. "And once it turns…"

Monika finished for him. "…it will face Earth."

Kai folded his hands behind his back. "And its descent trajectory will be set."

Inside, the observatory lights dimmed automatically. Screens glowed with pale gold reflections. The main spectrum display vibrated with a new pulse—deeper, slower, like the drumbeat of something ancient awakening from slumber.

Monika moved toward the console, breathing carefully. Her chest tightened — not with pain, but pressure. Like an invisible field was widening inside her.

Nilas touched her arm. "Sit. You're shaking."

She sank into the chair, exhaling. "It's resonating too strong tonight."

Kai stepped beside her, placing two fingers above her sternum. Not touching — aligning.

"You are entering the attunement threshold," he said softly.

Nilas sat on her other side. "What does that mean?"

Kai looked at him gently. "It means her soul-field is synchronizing with the object."

Nilas paled. "Is that dangerous?"

"No," Kai said. "But it requires support."

Monika opened her eyes, meeting Nilas's gaze. "I can feel it. Like something inside me is remembering itself."

Nilas reached for her hand without thinking. As she allowed it, something shifted between them.

Feelings. Soft. Warm. Certain.

Not romantic in the simple human sense — but ancient. A recognition that bypassed time.

Kai's voice softened. "The two of you have walked this cycle before."

Nilas's heart skipped a beat. "What cycle?"

"The cycle of awakening," Kai said.

Monika whispered, "I know."

Nilas stared at her, wondering why he was trembling. "How can you possibly know that?"

She placed her free hand atop his. "Because when you touched me… it felt like coming home."

Nilas closed his eyes, overwhelmed by a rush of warmth that wasn't emotion — it was memory. "I felt it too."

Kai stepped back with a knowing smile. "You are aligning. Equal resonance. Equal yoke."

Nilas whispered, "This… this has happened before?"

Kai nodded. "In another lifetime. Another turning."

Monika squeezed Nilas's hand. "We'll understand more soon."

The screens flickered violently. All three turned toward the central display. The harmonic spectrum had exploded into a series of rising arcs —seven arcs, layered atop one another, glowing gold, rose and fading into indigo.

Nilas whispered, "Seven again…"

Kai nodded. "Completion. Turning."

The object pulsed — a deep, resonant wave that shook the floor. Monika gasped, gripping Nilas's hand harder. "It's pulling on me…"

Nilas steadied her. "I've got you."

Kai stepped closer. "It is not pulling. It is aligning."

Another pulse. Stronger.

Monika's vision blurred — spirals of light filling her mind. "I see... the Arc," she whispered. "The curve... the fissure... opening toward—"

The screens flashed. The object's fissure rotated several degrees —clear, deliberate, irreversible.

Nilas stood up abruptly. "It's turning!"

Monika's breath hitched. "Toward Earth."

Kai nodded with solemn certainty. "The descent pathway has begun."

A deep vibration spread through the room, shaking the air itself; not violently, but with the force of something enormous shifting across the fabric of space.

Nilas grabbed Monika's shoulders, steadying her as her whole body resonated. She gasped, tears glistening in her eyes. "It's inside me," she whispered. "The turn. I can feel it."

Kai placed a hand above her head, guiding her through the resonance.

"You are attuning to its memory. Not its motion."

Nilas whispered, voice breaking: "What do we do? How do we help her?"

Kai smiled softly. "You don't stop it. You support it."

Monika looked at Nilas, breath trembling. Don't let go."

Smiling reassuringly, he whispered, "I won't,"

Kai stepped back, letting the alignment unfold.

Monika's body relaxed slowly, breath by breath, until the vibration eased and her mind cleared.

The screens stabilized. The object now *faced Earth.*

Nilas held her tightly, forehead against hers, breath unsteady.

"Monika... are you all right?"

She nodded slowly. Then whispered: "I remember him."

Nilas froze. "Me?"

"Yes," she whispered. "I remember you."

Kai turned away to give them privacy, though he remained silently present.

Nilas took her face gently in his hands. "From where?"

Monika closed her eyes, voice trembling. "From before."

Nilas swallowed hard, tears falling freely. "Monika, I…"

Before he could finish, the screens pulsed again — a soft, golden glow breathing through the observatory like an exhale.

Kai turned back. "It is done," he said. "The object has turned."

Nilas looked at him, eyes wide. "What happens now?"

Kai answered quietly, "Now it begins its descent."

Monika whispered, "And humanity's remembering begins with it."

Nilas held her close.

Outside, across the vast cold expanse of space, the object began the long, deliberate, descent arc toward Earth.

Caught At The Edge

CHAPTER 16

The Descent Begins

Outside, across the vast cold expanse of space, the object began the long, deliberate descent arc toward Earth. The alert arrived first in Chile.

Juan Alvarez had been awake for nearly twenty-six hours when the priority signal cut through the noise of routine telemetry. It was not flagged as anomalous. It was flagged as *verified*. He leaned closer to the screen, heart pounding as the confirmation cascade locked in—trajectory, velocity, rotational coherence, descent arc. There was no margin left for doubt.

Juan did not hesitate. He forwarded the report to Geneva and Hawaii simultaneously, tagging it with a designation that had not been used in decades:

Global Impact Advisory — Non-Natural Object.

Minutes later, in a glass-walled conference room overlooking Lake Geneva, Marc Trembly stood beside Professor Henri Duval as the alert populated across the main display.

Marc read it once. Then again. Then he felt his mouth go dry. He turned the screen slightly toward Henri and said carefully, "It's confirmed."

Henri did not move at first. He was staring at the projection, jaw clenched, fingers digging into the edge of the table as if the data itself were a provocation. "Confirmed *what*," Henri snapped.

Marc swallowed. "The descent arc. The rotational lock. The non-random coherence." He hesitated, then finished quietly. "It's deliberate."

That was when Henri exploded. "This is hysteria dressed as math," he barked, slamming his palm against the table. "We have seen this before. Comets. Debris. Statistical clustering. In 2013—" His voice rose. "—in this same region, we watched the sky fall and the world survived."

Marc held his ground. "This is not 2013."

Henri spun on him. "You think I don't know that? You think I don't understand what this *implies*?"

His breathing had grown shallow, uneven. "Geneva lies within the projected uncertainty cone. France borders it. My country borders it."

The room felt suddenly too small.

Marc lowered his voice. "Juan's data aligns with Hawaii and Germany."

At the mention of Germany, Henri's eyes flashed. "Frederick," he sneered. "Always eager to romanticize anomalies."

"This isn't romance," Marc said. "It's convergence."

Henri laughed sharply, a brittle sound with no humor in it. "You want to know what this really is?" He jabbed a finger at the screen. "It's impotence. We are watching something we cannot stop. Seventeen million miles away and not a single technology on this planet capable of touching it." The words hung in the air like poison.

Marc felt a chill run through him—not from fear, but from recognition. This was not a scientific argument anymore. This was terror.

In Hawaii, Reza Karimi was already pulling together a secure channel. Fifty people moved through the observatory with controlled urgency, voices low, systems synchronized. Kai stood apart from the activity, eyes closed for ~~a brief moment~~ a moment, as if listening beyond the instruments.

When the Geneva feed came online, Henri's voice filled the room before anyone could greet him. "You are making this worse," Henri accused. "By indulging this narrative. By allowing non-scientific personnel into critical interpretation."

Reza's expression hardened. "Monika Adler is here by invitation," he said evenly. "And by results."

Henri scoffed. "She is not a scientist."

Kai opened his eyes. "No," he said calmly. "She is not."

Marc watched from Geneva as the silence stretched.

Then Kai added, quietly, "And that is why she can remain aligned."

Marc felt something inside him shift. Not belief. Capacity.

Henri did not hear it that way. "This is madness," he said, pressing a hand to his chest now, breath uneven. "You are asking the world to *submit*."

"No," Kai replied. "We are asking it to listen."

The call ended badly. Henri remained standing long after the screens went dark, staring at the reflection of his own face in the glass wall, pale, rigid, furious.

Marc watched him, suddenly afraid. Not of the object. But of what resistance was doing to the human body.

Within hours, the world began to feel it. Not through instruments at first, but through instinct.

Markets wavered without clear cause. Emergency briefings were convened before formal alerts were issued. Military analysts found themselves awake long past midnight, rereading trajectory reports they did not yet trust. Something was changing, and no one wanted to be the first to say it aloud. By morning, the data caught up to the feeling.

Across international observatories, the same conclusion surfaced independently, the object was no longer in passive approach. Its orientation had shifted. Its trajectory had stabilized. Descent parameters were forming. Quiet confirmations moved through encrypted channels, through secure calls and emergency protocols never meant to be used together.

In Geneva, Henri' stood rigid before a wall of projected data, his jaw clenched so tightly it ached.

He did not sit. He could not. The city outside the window was still asleep, unaware of how close history had moved toward it.

"This region again," he said sharply, stabbing a finger at the display. "The same corridor." No one answered immediately.

Henri' turned, anger flashing beneath the fear he refused to name. "You remember 2013," he snapped. "The atmospheric strike. Same sector. Same gravitational channel. That event alone disrupted air traffic, seismic readings, communications. And that was small. That was *natural*." He leaned forward, palms flat on the table. "This is not."

The projection rotated, the descent arc passing uncomfortably close to Europe's upper latitudes. Geneva sat too near the margins of probability. France closer still.

Henri' swallowed hard. "If this object continues on its present course, the consequences will not be regional," he said. "They will be continental. Possibly global."

Someone on the call attempted reassurance. "We don't yet know impact parameters—"

"We know enough," Henri' cut in. "We know it is controlled. We know it is descending, and we know," his voice rose, "that we have no means to stop it."

That was the sentence that broke the room.

No weapons system could reach out seventeen million miles with precision. No propulsion system could intercept. No detonation—conventional or nuclear—could meaningfully alter its course at that distance. Every solution Henri' had ever trusted failed under the same arithmetic. His authority, his certainty, his science—all suddenly insufficient. "This must be neutralized," he said, voice tight. "I don't care how."

Silence answered him.

In that silence, fear took root—not only in Henri', but across a world that was beginning to understand it was no longer observing a phenomenon. *It was being approached.*

The world felt different the moment the object turned. Not because anything visible shifted, no tremors in the ground, no streaks of fire across the heavens, but because something subtle had tightened, as if the space between moments had drawn inward—breath, a pressure a quiet, unignorable recognition.

Monika sensed it first. A low, steady hum gathered beneath her sternum, deeper than any resonance she had known before. It was not urgent, not sharp—but deliberate, as though her inner field had been gently rotated to match a new orientation.

She stood at the observatory console, her hair tucked neatly behind one ear, posture immaculate as always. Yet beneath the composed exterior, something inside her felt newly exposed—raw and luminous at the same time.

Nilas sat beside her, tall frame folded forward, hair falling into those deep blue eyes that missed very little. His hands were wrapped around a mug of tea he did not remember lifting. He watched her breathing.

"Is it stronger?" he asked quietly.

Monika nodded, eyes still on the rising harmonic curve. "It's not a call this time," she said. "It's… presence."

Kai stood near the far observation window, framed by the palest light of dawn. His dark Polynesian features were calm, carved into stillness, but the air around him seemed subtly altered as though it carried a charge no instrument could detect. "It has begun its descent arc," he said.

Nilas frowned. "But it's still far. Millions of miles."

Kai did not look away from the sky. "In distance, yes. In resonance, no."
Monika drew another data stream onto the screen. The object's axis had fixed into a precise orientation—directly toward Earth. Its velocity had shifted as well. Not random. Not drifting. "It's slowing," she whispered.

Nilas blinked. "Slowing? Why would anything entering the solar system slow down?"
Kai stepped closer, folding his hands behind his back. "Because it is preparing for controlled entry."

The word *controlled* detonated across the Geneva channel. Henri Duval surged forward in his chair, color draining from his face. "Controlled?" he snapped. "You are describing impact using euphemism."

Marc saw it then—not intellectual resistance, but raw fear tightening Henri's jaw, sharpening his breath into short, shallow pulls.

"You are telling us," Henri continued, voice rising, "that an object seventeen million miles away is executing intention—and that we are expected to *allow* it."

No one answered immediately.

Henri's hand trembled as he braced himself against the table. "Do you have any concept of what happens if that trajectory shifts by fractions? Geneva lies inside the uncertainty cone. France borders it."

He laughed once, harsh and brittle. "We remember 2013. We remember how far-reaching that shockwave was. And this—" he gestured violently at the screen, "—this is not debris."

Nilas stared at him. "That means it's navigating."

"Yes," Kai said.

The truth settled into the room without spectacle. Monika swallowed. "It's choosing where to descend."

The World Begins to Feel It

As dawn spread across the mountains, messages began to surface from around the world. People waking with images they could not explain—curves, spirals, intersecting arcs. Children saying the air felt different, as though it carried a sound inside it.

Elders describing an unfamiliar stillness, neither fear nor peace. Animals pausing at horizons, attentive in ways that defied instinct.

Nilas scrolled through the feeds, his throat tightening. "People feel it everywhere," he said. "Every continent."

Kai inclined his head. "Because the object is no longer observing."

Monika felt the truth sharpen inside her. "It's interacting."

"Yes," Kai said simply.

On the screen, the harmonic pattern evolved into a double spiral—two arcs threading through one another with uncanny precision.

Nilas leaned closer. "I've seen that shape. Where?"

"In the Arc," Monika said. "In the visions."

Kai nodded. "It is revealing the structure of the descent field—the energy it will carry into Earth's magnetic grid."

Nilas froze. "You mean it's going to merge with Earth's field?"

"Yes."

Monika's breath caught. "That changes everything."

"It must," Kai said. "The planet cannot remain untouched."

Nilas hesitated. "The *Great Reset*—the Aries alignment on February twentieth…"

Kai nodded slowly. "The timing is not accidental."

Monika looked back at the screen. "So…the object isn't random."

"No," Kai said. "It is intentional."

Nilas set his jaw. "Then why Earth?"

Kai's gaze softened, though he did not answer immediately. "Because Earth is responsive."

The Message Arrives

A tremor passed through Monika's chest. She stiffened. "Kai."

Nilas was already beside her. "Monika—are you all right?"

"It's aligning with me again."

Kai raised a hand just above her sternum, attuning to something invisible. "Your perceptual field is shifting," he said. "You're translating coherence."

Monika closed her eyes as another wave rose through her—not words, not images, but a dense, golden knowing.

Nilas held her hands, grounding her.
"What do you sense?"

She inhaled slowly. "It's indicating where the descent will concentrate."

Kai leaned closer. "Where?"

"The north," she said.

Nilas whispered, "The Arctic."

"Yes. Near the Barents Sea." Kai exhaled, not in triumph, but acknowledgment. "A controlled approach."

Nilas's voice shook. "You knew."

"I sensed a range," Kai said. "Not a point."

Monika opened her eyes. "It chose a region where the disruption will be minimal."

Nilas pressed his lips together. "It's... careful."

Kai did not correct him. "It is precise."

The Field Activates

The screens pulsed once, then again, the tone deepening into a low, golden frequency that seemed to hum through the floor.

Nilas steadied Monika as she absorbed the resonance. "It's intensifying the field," she said. "Preparing the planet."

Kai nodded. "To soften the transition."

Nilas stared at the glowing arc. "What happens next?"

Kai answered without drama. "The world will register it."

Monika whispered, "And so will we."

Outside, dawn broke fully over the mountains, while far above Earth, the object adjusted its trajectory—not falling, not accelerating. Just moving with measured intent, as though crossing a boundary no instrument could yet define.

The descent had begun.

Caught At The Edge

CHAPTER 17

The Impact Over the Barents Sea

The world felt it before it saw anything.
Not as fear. Not as noise. But as pressure—subtle, electric, unmistakable—like the pause just before lightning breaks the sky. Across continents and time zones, people slowed mid-step. Conversations faltered. Animals grew still. Even the atmosphere seemed to hold itself in suspension, as though the planet were listening. Within hours, independent observatories across Europe, South America, and the Pacific reached the same conclusion: the object had committed to a descent path.

In Geneva, the confirmation did not register as discovery. It registered as danger.

Henri' stood rigid at the projection table, eyes locked on the descent model rotating above the glass. The vector was precise. Too precise. The corridor of influence swept uncomfortably close to Western Europe, brushing France's eastern boundary before curving north. Not an impact zone, but worse. A destabilization arc.

"This is not speculative," he said, his accent hardening. "This is a repeat pattern." He brought up an archived simulation and overlaid it without asking permission. A smaller event. A shorter arc. Less energy.

"Two thousand thirteen," Henri' said, "and this object carries orders of magnitude more coherence. Atmospheric coupling alone could fracture systems across the continent." He turned to the room, anger now bleeding through restraint. "You are telling me there is nothing we can intercept."

At the Hawaii observatory, Monika felt the shift strike her body with sudden clarity. A sharp thread of resonance traveled down her spine and settled beneath her sternum, luminous and steady. The same point that had responded since the night of the Arc. She did not gasp. She did not panic. She recognized it. "It's turning," she said.

Nilas was already beside her, his hand gripping the edge of the console. "Turning how?"

"Toward us," she replied.

Kai stood near the observation window, framed by the pale light of approaching dawn. His posture was calm, but the air around him carried a charge that instruments could not register. "It has begun its descent," he said.

Nilas shook his head. "That's not possible. It's still millions of miles out."

Kai did not look away from the sky. "In distance, yes. In resonance, no."

Monika's fingers moved across the display, calling up the latest trajectory data. The object's velocity curve was changing, flattening, adjusting, slowing in a way that defied every expectation of inertial motion. "It's decelerating," she whispered.

Nilas stared at the screen. "Why would anything slow down at this point?"

Kai answered without hesitation. "Because it is preparing for controlled entry." His words settled heavily in the room.

Monika swallowed. "It's choosing."

"Yes," Kai said. "Where. How. With whom it will interact."

Nilas scrolled through the incoming messages, his breath shallow. "They feel it everywhere."

Kai nodded. "Because the object is no longer observing."

Monika closed her eyes briefly as another wave passed through her chest; warm, precise, undeniable. "It's interacting," she said. She reopened the display and froze. The object's axis had locked into a fixed orientation. Directly toward Earth.

Then the images arrived. Satellites over the northern hemisphere captured the first clear visuals as the object crossed above the Arctic Circle; a luminous arc of structured light cutting through the upper atmosphere.

It did not burn. It did not fragment. It glowed. Gold. Copper. Rose. Emerald. Not chaotic color but ordered emission—harmonics made visible.

Nilas stared, his voice barely audible. "It's choosing the water."

Monika nodded. "The Barents Sea."

Kai confirmed it. "Far enough from land to spare millions. Close enough to ignite the planetary grid."

"Ignite what?" Nilas asked.

"The resonance field," Kai said. "The new frequency."

The cameras shook; not from turbulence, but from interference as the atmosphere responded. Spirals and lattices of light unfolded around the object, not as decoration, but as structure. Geometry alive with intention.

Monika felt tears slide down her cheeks without sadness. "It's working with the planet," she said. "Synchronizing with the planet's magnetics."

Nilas turned to her sharply. "How do you know?"

She pressed her palm to her chest. "Because it's synchronizing with us."

The descent accelerated—not violently, but decisively. Then, without warning, the object exhaled. A vast wave of luminous vapor burst outward, washing across the Arctic sky like a sunrise unfolding in every direction at once. The light carried no heat. No sound. Only resonance.

Nilas gasped. "Oh my God."

Monika whispered, "It's opening the chamber."

Kai nodded. "The descent seal."

The object met the Barents Sea not with an explosion, but with a sound so deep it felt like the lowest note of a cosmic instrument; felt more than heard. Water did not erupt. It rose. A column of light spiraled upward from the surface, gold and translucent, as the sea itself responded. Not resisting, not yielding, but participating.

In Geneva, alarms finally broke the spell. They were not sirens. They were system failures—screens lagging, feeds desynchronizing, instruments struggling to reconcile what they were recording with what should have been possible.

Henri' stood rigid at the center console, hands braced against the edge, his breath coming too fast. "This is not controlled entry," he snapped. "This is mass displacement. You do not *ease* into an ocean at that velocity."

His assistant, Marc Trembly, stood beside him, one hand resting on the back of Henri's chair, eyes fixed on the data streams cascading into incoherence. "The sea didn't resist," Marc said quietly. "It responded."

Henri' turned on him. "Do not anthropomorphize physics." His voice cracked. "You remember 2013? Chelyabinsk. One universal object, a fraction of this mass, and entire regions destabilized. This—" He gestured wildly at the screens. "—this borders my country."

His chest tightened. He pressed a hand against it, more in anger than fear. "We are watching extinction-level mechanics unfold without a single viable interception solution."

Marc did not argue. He stepped closer instead, steady, present, grounding. "Henri'. Breathe."

Henri' shook his head, eyes wild. "You cannot breathe through inevitability." Then he collapsed.

There was no warning. No gradual failure. One moment he was standing rigid before the screens, jaw clenched, eyes locked on the descending data stream; the next, his body folded inward as though the gravity he had been resisting all night had finally claimed him.

Marc was there instantly. He caught Henri' before his head struck the floor, lowering him carefully, one arm braced beneath his shoulders, the other pressed against his chest. Henri's breath came in sharp, shallow bursts, his eyes wide, not with pain, but with terror.

"It's too close," Henri' whispered. "This wasn't supposed to happen. We were supposed to stop it."

Marc leaned in, steady, voice low and calm. "You're safe. I've got you."

Henri' shook his head weakly. "You don't understand. Borders. Pressure waves. Cascades. This…this ends us."

His hand clawed at Marc's sleeve, desperate. His heart was racing against inevitability; a system locked in resistance with nowhere left to go.

Marc placed one hand firmly over Henri's sternum, the other cradling the back of his head. He did not argue. He did not explain. He did not correct. He grounded.

"Listen to me," Marc said softly. "Nothing is attacking you. Nothing is taking you."

Henri's breathing stuttered.

Marc stayed with him, breathing slow, deep, anchoring the space around them. The chaos of the lab faded. The alarms dimmed into background noise. For a moment—just a moment—Henri's body softened.

His eyes found Marc's. "I didn't want to be wrong," he whispered.

Marc nodded. "I know."

Henri' exhaled once—long, uneven—and did not draw another breath.

Marc did not move. He held Henri' as the last tension left his body, as fear released its grip, as the resistance that had defined his final hours finally gave way to stillness.

The monitors continued to scroll data, indifferent, precise. Around them, the Geneva lab fell silent. The sea did not erupt. It rose. A column of gold and translucent light spiraled upward, as though the planet itself were responding. Not resisting. Not yielding. Participating. A silent shockwave expanded outward—through Scandinavia, across Europe, Asia, Africa, the Americas. Not destructive. Not chaotic. Awakening.

In Hawaii, the observatory lights stabilized. Nilas dropped to his knees, overwhelmed. "This isn't an impact," he said hoarsely.

"No," Kai replied quietly. "This is activation."

Across the world, people felt it simultaneously: a loosening of fear, a sudden clarity, a stillness so profound it brought tears without sorrow.

Monika knelt beside Nilas, grounding him with her presence. "Breathe," she said softly. "Let it move through you."

He nodded, shaking. "What's happening to us?"

She answered without hesitation. "We're remembering."

Kai looked at the steady pulse on the screen. The Atlas, now at rest, aligned completely. He watched the data stabilize, the harmonic curves settling into coherence. "The descent is complete," he said. "The catalyst has entered Earth's field."

Nilas looked up at him, eyes wet. "What happens now?"

Kai turned toward the horizon, where the last of the light faded into ordinary dawn. "Now," he said, "the world must learn how to live with what it has become."

Monika felt the resonance beneath her sternum soften, no longer urgent, no longer pressing. It was simply *present*.

The old trajectory had ended. Nothing—no law, no institution, no fear, could return it. The impact had not shattered the world. "The world has crossed a threshold," he said quietly. It had changed its trajectory, and it will never return to what it was."

.

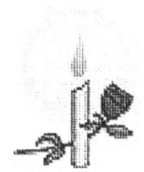

CHAPTER 18
The Day After

The first hours after the impact were strangely quiet. Not empty—quiet in the way a room feels after a long argument has ended, and no one yet knows what to say. Systems continued to function. Satellites remained in orbit. Power grids held. There were no sirens, no emergency broadcasts, no immediate instructions. Yet the world was not the same.

Monika noticed it in her body first. The pressure beneath her sternum, present for so long as tension and anticipation, had softened into a steady warmth. The resonance no longer pushed. It rested.

Nilas stood beside her, staring out the observation window as dawn fully broke over the mountains. His shoulders, usually held in careful readiness, had dropped. He exhaled slowly, as if realizing for the first time how tightly he had been holding himself together.

"I feel… lighter," he said, uncertain. "Is that possible?"

"Yes," Monika replied. "Because you're no longer bracing."

Kai remained still, observing not the screens, but the field itself—the subtle harmonics rippling through the space around them. "The planet has stabilized," he said. "The shock passed cleanly."

Nilas turned toward him. "People are going to expect chaos."

"They will find clarity instead," Kai said. "At least at first."

Across the world, the first reports arrived—not of damage, but of absence.

In Geneva, the absence was immediate and measurable. Three primary instruments went dark within minutes, not burned out, but inert—as if their sensing capacity had been quietly withdrawn. Marc Trembly stood alone at the central console, hands resting on cold glass, watching secondary systems struggle to compensate. He initiated a secure call without hesitation.

"Reza," he said when the line opened, voice steady despite the weight beneath it. "We've lost functional coherence here. Germany and Hawaii are still holding. I need to relocate—now."

The pause on the line was brief—measured, not uncertain.

"I agree," Reza said. "Geneva is too close to the interference field. We're seeing stabilization only in Hawaii and Bavaria. Hawaii is primary. We need someone who understands both systems and people."

He did not soften his voice. "Marc, we need you here."

Marc did not hesitate. He glanced once at the darkened Geneva displays, the instruments Henri' had trusted with his life's work.

"I'm on my way," he said.

Within the hour, Geneva classified the lab as non-operational. Civil transport was suspended across much of Northern Europe, but military corridors remained open. Marc boarded a quiet transport bound west, the aircraft lifting through cloud and static toward the Pacific.

As the lights of Europe fell away beneath him, Marc felt it—the same stillness others were beginning to name. Not belief. Not fear. Capacity.

Alignment was not something one argued with. It was something one arrived ready to hold.

As reports arrived from around the world, it was noted surprisingly that emergency rooms reported fewer admissions. Police scanners fell quiet. Financial markets paused, then reopened with unusual restraint, as if the impulse to panic had briefly gone missing.

In cities and villages alike, people stopped in the middle of ordinary actions—washing dishes, walking to work, standing in line—and felt a moment of inexplicable presence.

Not bliss. Not euphoria. Just *here*.

Children asked fewer questions and listened more. Animals moved calmly through spaces that once agitated them. Even the air seemed to carry sound differently—quieter~~softer~~, less cluttered.

Nilas scrolled through global feeds, his expression shifting from disbelief to something like awe.

"They're describing the same thing," he said. "All of them. Different words, same experience."

"What words?" Monika asked.

"Quiet," he said. "Clarity. Relief. Some people say it feels like the end of a long noise they didn't know they were hearing."

Monika nodded. "That noise was fear."

Kai added gently, "And separation."

As the hours passed, another pattern emerged. People began remembering.

Not memories in the usual sense—no sudden recall of past lives or hidden histories—but an internal reorientation. Old resentments loosened. Long-held arguments lost urgency. Decisions that once felt impossible resolved themselves without struggle.

Monika watched a replay of the harmonic data and realized something with a sudden certainty. "It didn't give us anything new," she said.

Nilas looked at her. "What do you mean?"

"It removed interference," she replied. "Like clearing static from a signal that was already there."

Kai inclined his head. "Yes. The catalyst did not install a future. It removed the weight of the past."

Nilas leaned back against the console, absorbing that. "So... this isn't the end of anything," he said.

"No," Monika replied. "It's the end of resistance."

Across the globe, grief and relief intertwined. Those who had lost loved ones in the first departures felt sorrow—but not confusion. The deaths made sense in a way death rarely did. There was no sense of abandonment. Only completion.

Nilas noticed it in himself too. The old urgency to explain, to frame, to publish before others could claim the narrative had gone quiet.

"For the first time," he said slowly, "I don't feel like I need to tell the world what happened."

Monika smiled faintly. "Because the world knows."

Kai stepped closer to the window, watching sunlight settle across the land. "The most difficult part comes next," he said.

Nilas frowned. "I thought this was it."

"This was the change," Kai replied. "Not the adjustment."

Monika felt the truth of it settle in her bones. "People will try to return to what they knew."

"Yes," Kai said. "Because familiarity feels safer than coherence at first."

Nilas nodded. "And institutions won't disappear overnight."

"No," Kai said. "But they will struggle to operate the same way."

As the day unfolded, humanity moved carefully, as if testing a new gravity. Arguments ended quickly. Lies felt heavy to speak. Silence carried information.

The world had not become perfect. It had become immediate.

That night, Monika slept without dreaming for the first time in months. Nilas sat beside her, watching the steady rise and fall of her breath, feeling no need to check the news.

Kai stood outside beneath the open sky, sensing the planet settle into its new rhythm.

The impact had passed. What remained was not instruction, not prophecy, not command. It was responsibility, and for the first time in human history, the weight of that responsibility did not feel unbearable.

It felt shared.

Caught At The Edge

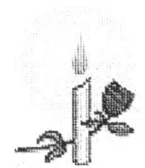

CHAPTER 19
Communities of Light

In the days following the descent, humanity did not rebuild the old world. It simply *walked out of it*. Not through revolt, not through collapse—but through an overwhelming inner clarity that made the old systems feel irrelevant, like a dream that no longer made sense upon waking.

People stopped clinging to what they once feared to lose. They followed a quiet, instinctive pull inside their chests...a vibration that guided them to one another.

Monika felt it first. Nilas felt it next. And soon— millions followed. Humanity began forming *Communities of Light*.

Not planned. Not organized. Not commanded. Just... *remembered*.

The Gathering

Three days after the descent, Monika stood on the ridge overlooking the valley below.

At dawn, a soft shimmer rose above the landscape—as if the Earth exhaled light instead of mist. Families walked in small clusters along newly forming paths, guided by intuition rather than instruction.

Karolin appeared along one of those new paths, walking with the same quiet steadiness she had shown on the mountaintop two days earlier. Her presence was unmistakable, even from afar. Nilas saw her first—he knew the way she held her shoulders, the way her gaze softened when she took in the world. He inhaled sharply, relief flooding him so suddenly that his eyes stung. Karolin met his gaze across the distance and smiled, the kind of smile that carried both old grief and new belonging.

Without words, she drifted toward the gathering, instinctively helping disoriented families and calming those overwhelmed by their heightened senses. She fit into the new world as though she had always been shaped for it.

Nilas joined her, touching her arm lightly. "You see it, don't you?" he whispered.

Monika nodded. "They're finding each other."

Soul families. Resonant groups. Not by blood or language or history—but by vibration.

Kai came to stand between them, watching the movement below with quiet reverence. "The old world grouped people by geography," he said. "The new world groups them by resonance."

Nilas exhaled. "It's so… natural."

"It is the way of awakened planets," Kai replied.

The First Circles

In the valley, small circles formed. Each circle contained eight to twelve people— different ages, backgrounds, former beliefs—yet each group shared a harmonized emotional field.

They didn't need to speak to understand each other. They didn't need to explain why they were drawn together. They simply felt: *This is mine. This is home. These are my people.*

People whose frequencies matched.

Karolin moved easily among them, her clinical intuition blending seamlessly with the new resonance. Her years of psychological training at Pepperdine had given her a deep understanding of emotional landscapes, but here, in this softened world, her gifts expanded naturally. People gravitated toward her without knowing why, sensing her calm presence as a steadying force in the rising frequency.

Monika stepped closer to the gathering. A group of children sat together on the ground—some drawing spirals in the soil, others humming harmonics that matched the wind.

Nilas whispered, "They're using the new resonance already."

Kai nodded. "Children adapt first. They remember faster."

A little girl turned and looked directly at Monika. Not curious. Not startled. Recognizing. Monika felt the same recognition pulse in her chest. "She knows me," Monika whispered.

"She remembers your field," Kai said. "In the new frequency, memory is not limited to the past."

Nilas chuckled softly. "So… reincarnation is basically an open book now."

Kai smiled. "Something like that."

The Teaching Fields

As more people gathered, natural roles emerged. Not hierarchies. Not authority. Simply resonance. Some felt drawn to tending the land—touching seeds, feeling the Earth respond beneath their fingers.

Some began healing others—placing their hands on shoulders, chests, foreheads—energies aligning like ripples in a pond.

Others were teachers. Not of information—but of remembrance. Kai, unsurprisingly, became a teacher of the children.

They flocked to him. They sat in circles around him, eyes wide, hearts open, energy coherent.

Nilas whispered, "What is he teaching them?"

Monika listened.

Kai spoke not of facts, but of natural law: "Feel the field before your move."
"Listen to the silence behind the sound."
"Your thoughts are wind; your heart is the mountain."
"Do not seek power — seek alignment."

It was simple. It was profound. It was exactly what the new children needed.

Monika felt tears rise. "This is what the world was missing," she said softly. "A foundation."

Nilas nodded. "A soul foundation."

The Harmony Centers

By the end of the first week, the communities had formed harmonic centers. Open spaces where people gathered at sunset: to meditate, to share food, to sing in spontaneous resonance, to rest in silence.

Light rose naturally from the ground—a faint glow—not electricity, but resonance made visible.

Nilas watched the center fill with people, bathed in subtle golden radiance. "This is what Earth looks like healed," he whispered.

Monika squeezed his hand. "This is what it looks like when humanity remembers itself."

Kai joined them, a serene warmth in his eyes. "In the old world, people chased safety," he said. "In the new world, safety grows from unity."

Nilas smiled at him. "You knew this was possible?"

"Possible?" Kai echoed. "It was inevitable."

Monika's Realization

That night, as the community sang low harmonic tones that vibrated through the Earth, Monika felt something new awaken inside her. A soft pulse. A quiet expansion. A sense of... belonging.

Nilas turned to her, sensing the shift. "What is it?"

Monika took his hand and pressed it to her abdomen. "I'm part of this world now. Not just observing it. Not translating it. *Belonging to it.*"

Nilas pulled her close. "You always did," he whispered.

Kai watched them, a gentle smile touching his lips. "The Communities of Light are forming," he said. "And soon... they will unify."

Monika exhaled knowingly. "And then?"

Kai looked toward the horizon, where the soft light shimmered like a promise. "Then the resonance will rise again, and the next phase will begin."

Monika leaned into Nilas, the song of the community surrounding them like a warm embrace. The old world had ended. Something far more magnificent had begun.

Caught At The Edge

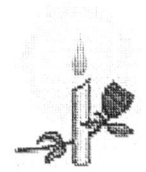

CHAPTER 20
The Still Point

After the upheaval came a pause. Not silence in the ordinary sense, but a deep settling—as if the world, having exhaled, did not yet inhale again. Movement slowed. Not everywhere, not uniformly, but perceptibly. The frantic edge that had driven action for generations seemed to dull, replaced by a strange attentiveness. People noticed things they had long overlooked: the weight of a moment, the tone beneath words, the consequence hidden inside intention.

Nothing new had been announced. Nothing had been decided—yet something fundamental had reasserted itself. In the absence of noise, patterns became visible. Effort no longer produced the same results it once had. Force met resistance.

Precision met ease. When actions were taken in fear, they unraveled quickly. When taken in clarity, they seemed to hold. It was not punishment. It was feedback.

Cause and effect moved closer together, as though distance itself had collapsed. Choices carried weight sooner. Silence carried meaning. Stillness revealed information faster than urgency ever had.

Some found the pause unsettling. Mistaking it for emptiness and rushed to fill it—only to discover that haste now worked against them. Others sensed relief without understanding why, as if a pressure they had never named had finally lifted.

The world was not asking to be fixed. It was asking to be acknowledged. Beneath politics, beneath belief, beneath language itself, something older than instruction had resumed its place. A coherence that required no enforcement. A balance that could not be commanded, only respected. This was not a new order imposed from above. It was the return of proportion.

The laws that govern alignment had never vanished; they had simply been obscured. Now, with the field cleared, they surfaced quietly—like bedrock revealed when floodwaters recede.

Nothing had been promised. Nothing had been guaranteed, but the strain of maintaining distortion had eased. The world grew *still* enough to receive what could only arrive in such a space.

At the *still point*, creation does not rush.
It waits.

Caught At The Edge

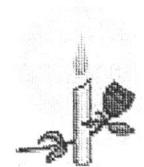

CHAPTER 21

Love Incarnates and Life Continues

Love did not arrive with ceremony. It arrived quietly, not as an ending or a beginning, but as love taking form once more—without announcement, without force, without the need to be witnessed by anyone beyond those who were present.

In the weeks after the Still Point, as the world learned how to move again without friction, Monika and Nilas found themselves standing together more often in silence than in conversation. The urgency that had once defined their days was gone. What remained was something steadier—truer.

They walked the shoreline at dusk, the ocean calm, the air warm with salt and wind. The world no longer pressed. It breathed.

Nilas stopped once and turned to her, studying her face as if seeing it for the first time without the overlay of crisis. "This isn't an ending," he said softly.

Monika shook her head. "No. It's a beginning that doesn't need permission."

They married without spectacle. No audience. No declarations meant for history. Just the sound of waves and the quiet presence of those who mattered.

Karolin stood beside Monika, her hands steady, her eyes clear. Marc stood with Nilas, grounded, solid, already bonded to him in a way neither of them needed to explain. The connection between them had been immediate upon Marc's arrival in Hawaii—not forged by shared trauma, but by shared steadiness. Brothers not by blood, but by alignment.

Dr. Reza stood at the altar, calm and steady, his voice carrying the quiet authority of one who understood both science and soul. A former Navy captain, licensed long ago to perform marriages, he carried authority without display—accustomed to responsibility, yet unburdened by ceremony. There was no pretense in him—only reverence. He spoke not of binding, but of recognition.

Kai walked Monika forward.

Not as escort alone, but as one who had traveled beside her across thresholds few could name. His presence was grounding, ancient, and deeply familiar. When he released her hand, it was with the unspoken knowing that she no longer needed guidance—only choice.

Monika felt Frederick's absence—but not as loss. He was present in another way now, woven into the moment rather than missing from it. What had been fulfilled no longer needed to stand beside her. Love had already done its work.

Marc stood with Nilas, steady and loyal, a quiet strength at his side. This was not the gathering of strangers, but of those who had survived something together—who understood what it meant to arrive here.

The air itself seemed to pause. This was not a beginning. It was an arrival.

During the ceremony Monika felt Frederick's presence. She felt him in the way one feels a father who trusts the world enough to let his child step fully into it.

Frederick had returned to Germany weeks earlier. His station required him. His family was there. The world had not stopped needing structure simply because it had learned coherence.

His message had arrived the night before the ceremony—brief, warm, unmistakably his.

You are not leaving anything behind, he wrote. *You are stepping into it. When the child is born, come to Germany. Stay as long as time allows. There are places that remember love across centuries.* He had signed it simply:
Always,
F.

After the ceremony, they sat together on the sand as twilight folded into night. There was no urgency to speak. No need to name what had already settled.

It was Karolin who noticed first. Monika's hand rested unconsciously at her abdomen, her breath slower, deeper. Karolin met her eyes, a quiet understanding passing between them. "It's early," she said gently, "but it's clear."

Nilas looked between them, then back to Monika. She nodded.

Joy did not explode. It unfolded.

Michael was born just before dawn, a few months later, the air still, the world holding its breath in a way that no longer felt ominous.

Karolin guided the birth with calm certainty, her hands sure, her presence unwavering. Something in her shifted as her nephew entered the world—not ascension, not transformation, but anchoring. Her frequency did not rise away from the Earth. It rooted into it.

Michael did not cry immediately. He opened his eyes.

Nilas felt it then—the moment the future stopped being abstract. He pressed his forehead to Monika's, breath breaking, grounding himself in the weight of what had arrived. "This is what it was all for," he whispered.

"No," Monika said softly. "This is what it continues as."

In Germany, Frederick stood on a balcony overlooking the Isar river. As dawn touched the stone bridges, the Isar's alpine waters were quietly flowing north from the Alps. He felt the birth without being told. The same way he had always known when Monika crossed a threshold. He smiled, placed a hand over his heart, bowed his head and whispered, *"Welcome."*

Life did not wait for the world to agree. Children were being born everywhere—quietly, steadily—into a reality that did not demand belief, only presence.

Love had incarnated not as myth, not as promise, but as continuity. The future, no longer distant or theoretical, breathed softly in the arms of those ready to hold it.

CHAPTER 22
The Council of Nine

The call did not arrive as sound or signal. It arrived as recognition.

Across the world, people felt a quiet inward pull—subtle, steady, unmistakable. Not urgency. Not command. A knowing. As if something ancient had reached the surface again and was ready to be acknowledged.

The gathering did not begin with a summons. There was no announcement made, no message sent through any system old or new. People arrived because something inside them said *now*. Not urgently. Not fearfully. Simply with certainty.

They came from nearby valleys and distant towns, on foot and by quiet transport, alone and in small groups. No one asked who had organized it. No one checked credentials. No one stood at the edge to direct movement. The land itself seemed to know where people belonged. The clearing filled slowly.

Not densely. Not chaotically. People spaced themselves as if guided by an invisible intelligence, leaving room between bodies, between thoughts. Conversations were brief, then fell away. Children sat without being told. Elders stood without leaning, steady in their bodies. The air held a steady calm—not reverent, not tense—attentive.

Monika felt it as soon as she stepped into the field: a settling beneath her sternum, familiar and quiet. This was not the resonance of change. This was the resonance of *recognition*.

Nilas adjusted Michael against his chest. The child was awake, hazel eyes open, calm, alert—not searching the crowd, not startled by it. He simply observed.

Kai stood a short distance away, not apart, not central. Present without orientation. For the first time since the descent, his presence did not guide the field; it acknowledged it.

No one stood at the center. That was the first sign. In the old world, gatherings required a focal point—someone to begin, someone to claim attention. Here, the absence of that impulse went unnoticed. No one waited for instruction. No one grew restless. Time passed differently.

Then, without signal, the field shifted. It was subtle. A tightening—not of fear, but of coherence. Like threads drawing together without tension. People felt it in their chests, their spines, their breath. No one spoke. No one needed to.

One person stepped forward. Not dramatically. Not decisively. Simply because staying where they stood no longer made sense.

A woman whose hands had steadied others through the crossings moved into the open space and stopped. She did not face the crowd. She faced the ground. A moment later, another followed—a man whose presence quieted rooms long before he ever spoke. He stood several paces away, leaving space between them. Then another and another. Not in sequence. Not evenly spaced. Each arrival felt like the completion of something already forming.

A farmer whose attention aligned land and season. A scientist whose listening had outpaced his measuring. An elder who carried memory without nostalgia. A protector who understood restraint more deeply than force. A translator—of languages, of emotion, of inner weather. A young woman whose clarity did not seek recognition. Finally, Kai stepped forward—not as origin, not as authority, but as confirmation.

Nine stood in the open space. No one named them. No one applauded. The crowd did not lean forward. It exhaled.

Monika felt it then—not excitement, not relief—but a sober clarity settled across the field. This was not selection by preference. This was not leadership by aspiration. This was function revealed.

Nilas understood it instinctively. He did not think *leaders*. He thought *holders*. Michael lifted one small hand.

Nothing visible happened. No light. No sound. But the field stabilized.

People felt it as a weight evenly distributed, a balance restored. The old reflex—to look for direction, to ask what came next—failed to arise. Instead, something quieter took its place. *Responsibility*. Not imposed. Not assigned. Shared.

No oath was spoken. No role defined. The Nine did not turn to address the gathering. They remained oriented toward one another, as if the work itself required that posture.

The crowd did not wait for more. Slowly, naturally, people began to step back. Not dismissed. Complete. Conversations resumed in low tones. Families drifted together. Children stood and stretched.

The Nine remained until the space emptied, then dispersed without ceremony. There would be no elections. No campaigns. No transfer of power. The old world's question—*Who decides?* had dissolved.

Humanity realized it was no longer *caught at the edge.* In its place stood a truth long hidden, now revealed; it had stepped beyond survival and into conscious becoming.

Authority no longer arose from choice; it arose from coherence. The field held. The world had crossed another threshold, and this one could not be undone

Caught At The Edge

CHAPTER 23

For The Collective—The First Council of Unity

Humanity did not assemble itself through instruction. No one called it a council, but for the first time, humanity was unified in listening.

There was no summons, no signal sent across networks, no appointed place announced in advance. People arrived because they felt a gentle internal orientation—a pull that did not hurry them, did not command, but quietly aligned their steps.

No elections. No hierarchy. No confusion about power. This is the first true meeting of humanity after remembering.

Weeks passed. Not marked by deadlines or declarations, but by a steady recalibration of daily life. The world did not rush back into motion. It learned a different rhythm—one that allowed action without urgency and choice without pressure.

The Nine did not call the First Council of Unity. The people did. Not through demand or expectation, but through a shared readiness that surfaced gradually, unmistakably.

Communities had formed. Bonds had stabilized. Old fears had softened enough for something deeper to emerge: the desire to sit together without needing to be led.

When the gathering came, it felt nothing like the assemblies of the past. No banners. No podiums. No symbols of authority. People arrived with food, with children, with elders walking slowly at their sides. They came knowing they would not be told what to do—and no longer needing to be.

The valley opened easily, as if it had been waiting. Circles formed naturally, overlapping rather than rigid. No central ring. No raised space. The Nine were present but not elevated. They sat among the people, not apart from them, recognizable only by the steadiness of the field around them.

Monika felt it as soon as she stepped into the gathering: a sense of shared adulthood. Humanity was no longer asking to be governed. It was asking how to live together.

Nilas sat beside her, Michael asleep against his chest. Around them, people spoke quietly, sharing experiences rather than opinions.

"I stopped arguing," one man said softly. "Not because I was right—but because it wasn't worth the fracture." A woman nearby nodded. "I left my job. Not in anger. It just… didn't fit anymore."

Others spoke of forgiveness that arrived without effort. Of truths spoken gently and received without defense. Of grief still present but no longer isolating.

When the Nine spoke, it was not to direct the gathering. It was to listen aloud. One by one, people stood—not to demand answers, but to articulate what they were discovering.
"We don't need rules," an elder said slowly. "We need awareness."

"A structure still helps," another offered, "but only if it breathes."

A farmer added, "The land responds when we don't force it. So do people."

Silence followed—not awkward, not expectant. *Thoughtful.*

Then Kai spoke—not rising, not projecting, simply entering the field. "Unity is not sameness," he said. "And freedom is not absence of responsibility." He looked around the circle, meeting eyes without holding them. "The old world feared power because it was hoarded. This world dissolves power by sharing consequence."

No one argued. They felt the truth of it in their bodies. A young woman stood with a child on her hip. "So how do we decide things together?"

The question was honest. Unafraid.

Nilas answered before he realized he was speaking. "By listening until clarity replaces urgency." Heads nodded.

Monika added quietly, "And by stopping when it doesn't." Laughter moved through the circle—not humor, but relief.

By the end of the gathering, nothing had been voted on. No laws passed. No leaders appointed. No future outlined. Yet everyone left knowing exactly what to do next.

Care for what is dear. Speak only what is true. Act when aligned. Pause when uncertain.

The Nine did not close the council. The people did—by rising naturally. Conversations continuing as they walked, children running ahead, elders lingering to finish thoughts that no longer needed conclusion.

As twilight settled in, Monika watched the gathering dissolve into ordinary movement and felt something settle deeply inside her. "This is it," she said softly. "This is freedom."

Nilas nodded. "Not independence."

"No," she agreed. "Interdependence—without fear."

Michael stirred, opening his sleepy eyes briefly before settling down again.

The field responded, not dramatically, but warmly—as if acknowledging continuity rather than beginning. The Council of Unity had not created a new world; it had confirmed one. Humanity had not been given instructions. It had remembered how to stand together.

Caught At The Edge

CHAPTER 24

The Way Forward

Morning returned without announcement. The light rose as it always had—steady, impartial—touching rooftops, fields, oceans, and stone with the same patience it had offered for centuries. No color lingered in the sky where the Atlas had entered. No mark remained to prove what had happened, yet nothing was the same. Not elevated. Not charged. Simply… honest.

Monika noticed it first in her body. The familiar pressure beneath her sternum—once tension, once anticipation—had settled into warmth. Not directive. Not insistent. Just present. A quiet confirmation that something fundamental had aligned and would not be undone.

Nilas stood at the window, coffee forgotten in his hands, watching the street below. Neighbors moved more slowly. Not hesitantly—deliberately. Greetings lingered a moment longer than habit required. People met one another's eyes without bracing. "They're not rushing," he said.

Monika joined him. "They don't need to."

Kai stood a few steps back, listening more than watching. The field around him felt complete now—no longer guiding, no longer shaping. The work of arrival was finished. What came next belonged to human hands. "The world has entered responsibility," he said quietly. "Not instruction."

Nilas turned. "That sounds fragile."

Kai nodded. "It is. Which is why it matters." There were no announcements that day. No declarations. Governments still met. Institutions still functioned, but something beneath them had shifted. Decisions rooted in fear felt heavier to carry. Words spoken without truth landed awkwardly in the body. People noticed. Some tried to resurrect old certainty—old enemies, old noise, old urgency—but the effort exhausted them more quickly than before. The field no longer sustained what required denial.

Monika felt it when she tried to explain what had happened—and realized explanation diminished it. "So... we don't," she said finally.

Nilas nodded. "We live it."

Across the world, small choices began to accumulate. People listened longer before responding. Paused before reacting. Told the truth more often—not because it was demanded, but because falsehood felt cumbersome.

Work changed shape. Communities reorganized without slogans. Families renegotiated roles that no longer fit. Some relationships ended. Others deepened with unexpected ease. Nothing was perfect. Nothing was postponed.

Michael slept through most of it, as newborns do. His presence did not command attention, it anchored it. When he opened his hazel eyes, people softened without knowing why.

"He's not here to lead," Nilas said one afternoon, watching his son breathe.

"No," Monika replied. "He's here to remind."

Kai prepared to leave at dusk.

"Where will you go?" Nilas asked.

Kai smiled faintly. "Where I'm needed and where I'm not."

Monika met his gaze. "Will we see you again?"

"Yes," he said. "And no."

That night, the valley settled into ordinary darkness. Stars emerged—no brighter than before, no closer. The Earth turned. Time continued, but the margin for unconsciousness had narrowed. The future no longer waited to be predicted, saved, or explained. It waited to be met—moment by moment—by people willing to stand inside consequence without fear.

Monika closed the door and sat quietly, Michael warm, content, nursing against her chest. Nilas joined her. Neither of them spoke. There was nothing left to say.

Outside, the world continued. Not redeemed. Not condemned. But *Awake.* Lights moved across cities where strangers paused, uncertain why they felt less alone. A nurse lingered beside a patient a moment longer than required. A pilot altered course by instinct and avoided a storm he never saw. A child, somewhere, looked up at the night sky without fear for the first time.

No announcement marked the shift. No monument recorded it. The Earth turned as it always had. Yet something within humanity had crossed a line that could not be uncrossed.

Elizabeth Joyce

Not saved.
Not finished.
But begun.

This time, the remembering would not be forgotten.

Caught At The Edge

ABOUT THE AUTHOR

Elizabeth Joyce is an author whose work focuses on systems under stress—astronomical, technological, psychological, and institutional—and the moments when established models fail to explain emerging realities. Her writing is informed by long-term study of pattern recognition, convergence analysis, and the ways independent observers across disciplines arrive at the same conclusions before formal consensus is reached.

In *Caught at the Edge*, her first novel, Joyce applies a methodical, process-driven approach to discovery, emphasizing how anomalies are identified, tested, and either dismissed or validated through evidence rather than assumption. The novel reflects her interest in how professionals respond to data that resists existing frameworks, and how truth often emerges through repetition, corroboration, and delayed recognition.

Joyce's perspective is shaped by extensive research into astronomical observation, human decision-making under uncertainty, and the dynamics of complex systems approaching transition points. Her work avoids sensationalism in favor of precision, allowing tension to arise from implication, restraint, and consequence.

Joyce's perspective has been informed by personal encounters with disruption, recovery, and resilience—experiences that sharpened her focus on how humans respond when established frameworks no longer suffice. This grounding gives her work a restrained authority, allowing tension to build through implication and realism rather than exaggeration.

She lives and works in New Hampshire and continues to write fiction that explores what happens when technology, evidence, and human awareness converge—and when the cost of ignoring that convergence becomes irreversible.

E-mail: elizabeth@new-visions.com

24 hour Answering service: 201-934-8986

Made in the USA
Coppell, TX
22 February 2026

71866472R00132